Also by Laura Livingston Snyder

The Infinity Series
DREAM SEER
REALM SPEAKER

and

MEDITATIONS HANDBOOK:
Four Revelations of the Solar Wheel of Meditations,
Affirmations, and Guided Imagery for Pagan Sabbats

Infinity Series

Spell Breakers

Laura Livingston Snyder

ISBN: 978-1-7351913-3-1

Photography: Laura Livingston Snyder
Infinity Series logo photography: Anatoli Photograffi
Publisher: Laura Livingston Snyder
Publisher email: applesnyder6@gmail.com
Cover design and art design: Laura Livingston Snyder

For Steve,
My everything

A big thank you to
Alexandra Butterfield for editing and adding all those pesky
commas

Will's house Main level

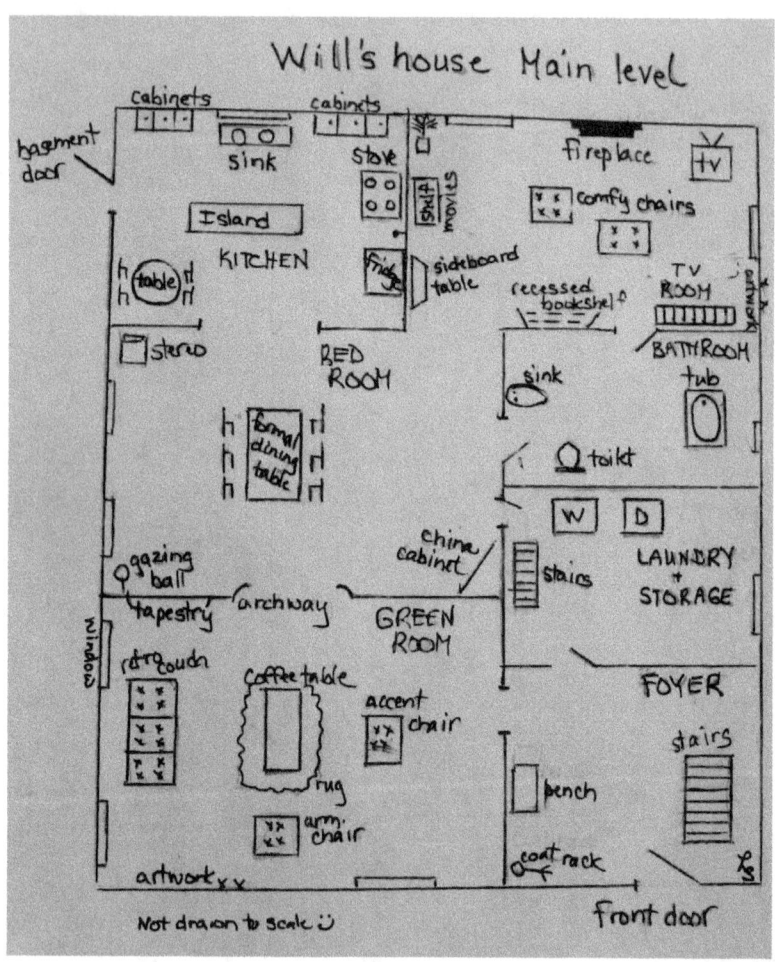

One

HE BLACK BLADE with the fine point shone in the concentrated flashlight beam. The fact that it was small, with a crooked wooden handle, proved that it had been Sylvia Cabet's athame. The fact that it had disappeared from the Sewing Room window and reappeared on the hidden altar within the last half hour proved Sylvia's prowess. Her power as a witch carried her spells not only beyond the realms, but a hundred and fifty years into the future. Impressive.

Will looked at Jenna before he took it off the altar. His expression wavered from wonder to an intensity Jenna couldn't quite pinpoint. Whatever it was, it made the sleeping Jenna uncomfortable. Will held it in his hand, looking up at Jenna, committing her to the secret only they knew...

JENNA STOOD OUTSIDE the entryway and took a deep breath, ignoring the condensation that swirled and merged into a diaphanous bubble by her mouth and nose. She knocked on the beautiful ornate door. It was six paneled with carved designs and appeared to be made of rich oak. The top of the door was rounded like an archway and the wrought iron handle and tacks gave it a gothic feel. The middle glass panels had a swirling lattice etching that distorted the image that grew in size the closer it came to Jenna. The door opened without the heft Jenna expected, and a familiar smile greeted her warmly.

"Merry meet, Jenna! Welcome to our home," Sulis said, wiping her hands on a dishtowel.

"Thank you," Jenna replied. She was nervous about what she would encounter in the private living space of her two favorite Pagans. This had been a long time coming. Will had been stubborn and adamant about Jenna not visiting his home until the majority of it had been renovated. Even though Jenna had said she didn't care, that it wasn't a reflection of their housekeeping skills if it was torn up to be rebuilt, Will wouldn't budge.

She had received an invitation from Will the second Friday of November while they were both watching television in the living room of her home. He had snuck a piece of paper folded into a greeting card size from his pocket to her hand. On the front, written in marker in Will's writing were block letters YOU ARE INVITED. On the inside was a simple message inviting her to a private open house at his place the next night for dinner. Her breathing hitched as she read the last line that said, "Love, Will."

Jenna walked into the foyer, and turned to shut the door

behind her. The handle was metal and heavy, but the door was light and smooth. It wasn't weighted like oak.

"Pretty isn't it? The real ones are outrageous in price. This is fiberglass, but it looks real enough, and adds to the feel of the period of the house." Sulis took her coat and hung it up on the tall coat rack by the door.

Jenna absentmindedly straightened the scoop neck of her white peasant shirt, and straightened the bottom hem over her black slacks. Even though it tended to pull down in the front, she liked the shirt because of its three tiny pearl buttons down the neckline, and matching pearl button at the bottom of the pleated cap sleeves.

She looked around eagerly, taking in the fresh lemony smell of cleanness. To the right was a long staircase to the second floor. A small, but sturdy bench with deep green cushions sat against the opposite wall. In the corner of the bench sat a small stuffed cat with funny eyes that made Jenna smirk.

"Make yourself at home. Will should be down shortly."

Jenna walked out of the foyer and into a large room, taking in the details that had occupied Sulis and Will's attention for months. The high ceilings were freshly painted in white down to the wainscoting, where the color changed to a spring green. A short, simple, wooden coffee table with a fluffy cream rug underneath sat in the middle of the room. It was surrounded by a retro style couch and chair set in a durable tapestry pattern with wooden arm rests that highlighted the polished hard wood floors. An accent chair with a high back was across from the couch. Three pieces of artwork—of winged faeries and goddesses—were majestically framed and adorned the walls.

A six-foot tapestry of a forest with knights and horses that looked very old, hung on another wall. Two windows, almost the length of the wall itself, were on the left. They were dressed in thick cream and white drapes with a jacquard pattern. There were no stereotypical caldrons and pointed hats.

"Wow, this is amazing, Sulis," Jenna whispered as she continued on.

Sulis smiled. "What's amazing is what you can find at estate sales, and how much you can save by doing the restoring on your own."

The green room ended in an archway into another main room of the same size. Jenna peeked around. She was not sure what this room was called. It, too, had vaulted white ceilings with detailed trim down to the wainscoting, where the lower half was a deep red. In the very middle was a beautiful dark wood formal dining table and chair set. There was a gazing ball in the corner on a wooden stand that was carved with intricate designs of stars and swirls. In the other corner was a very modern stereo system with a rack underneath for vinyl records and CD's. Along the same wall as the archway was an antique corner unit china cabinet next to a door Sulis opened. To the very right of them was a stairway. To the left, a utility room.

"This is our laundry room. These stairs lead to the opposite side of the second floor," Sulis pointed out. "The house is quite large. Although we've just renovated these rooms, we tried to retain the heritage."

"You have for sure. It has a nice homey feel."

Jenna faintly heard boots clunking down the stairs behind

her. She turned, just as Will became visible in the green room. Her face lit up as her stomach stirred with butterflies.

"Hi," Will's soft-spoken tone greeted her. She grinned back.

Jenna walked over and hugged him briefly, still not comfortable with public displays of affection, especially in front of his own mother. "Okay, I can see why you made me wait. This has an impressive "wow" factor. I am in awe." Will's face filled with pride.

"Well, we haven't had a chance to completely redo the house, but we're getting there," Sulis admitted, as she passed under the archway.

"The kitchen isn't done yet." Will placed his hand on the small of Jenna's back as they walked through the green and red rooms into a large kitchen. It was unfinished, but clean and neat, with a bright sunflower theme. Savory smells of tomatoes and garlic added a warm, inviting air to the large house. Directly in front of them was the sink and cupboards. To the left, was a dining area with a wooden table with four chairs. Sunflower candle holders with white tapers were opposite a flower arrangement centerpiece in a dark basket. Beyond the table was a thick farmhouse door with an apron hanging on a coat hook. A countertop island with cabinets below sat in the middle of room. Sulis put her dishtowel through the oven door handle and straightened it. It was yellow with sunflowers and bees. Over the stove there was a pull-string, but no light fixture above it.

"What's that for?" Jenna inquired.

"It was used like an intercom system a long time ago, for people in the basement."

"Why would you need an intercom?" Jenna asked, surprised. This was everything she loved about old and interesting.

"You haven't seen exactly how big this place is. And it's practically soundproofed. If I were to yell to you that dinner was ready, you'd be lucky to hear me in the green room, let alone downstairs," Will explained.

"Wow," was all Jenna could manage.

"This room is not nearly as big as the ones you just passed through, but Mom says it'll cost twice as much to restore as any of the others."

"Kitchens and bathrooms both," Sulis added ruefully. "Dinner will be ready in about twenty."

"Come on, I'll show you around."

Jenna shook her head a little, surprised at how she had arrived at this moment in time. Just two months ago she had met Will when he started to work with her at the Historical Association's museum. Jenna remembered the blood, sweat, and tears—literally and figuratively—she had shed in that building. That was the place where Jenna's gift for dream walking became apparent when she was only twelve. It also awoke her ability to channel unsettled spirits whose unfinished business prevented them from completely crossing over.

It was through these ordeals that Jenna—with her pals Tina and Toby—learned the building's second story window, in the Sewing Room, was a portal to the other side. It was the place where all the trouble began when the building was renovated. Those supernatural events came to a halt when the window closed on its own after two lost souls were reunited. They were Elizabeth and Joseph. Paranormal events started back up a few months ago, Jenna's junior year, just as she started her first real paying job: being the museum's first docent. And Will, who happened to adore her as much as she liked him, was the second hire.

"Just this way, Jenna," Will directed.

Jenna sighed, admiring her boyfriend as she followed through a doorway on the left into another smaller living room. This room was cozy, done all in neutrals, and had a fireplace on the far wall. The mantel held candelabras and knick-knacks of gray and black cats. Above it was a modest photograph of a family of three. The seated woman was a very young-looking Sulis, with wavy, shoulder length hair and large glasses. She was wearing a plain gray sweater dress with high boots. On her lap was a baby about a year old. The baby, in a powder blue jumper, stared with a perfect oval mouth, intrigued by what had caught his attention. Wispy, auburn hair not yet long enough to comb, covered his head. Behind them stood a man who looked a few years older than Sulis. He wore a white dress shirt and dark gray slacks with a light blue tie. He had a warm smile and seemed relaxed, with one arm around his wife, and one on his son's shoulder. The dark hair and brown eyes were the exact color of Will's.

"That was my dad, Brian. He died a few months after this portrait was taken."

Jenna's stomach tightened. She wanted to console him but wasn't sure if that would be appropriate. She had little experience with death other than when Mrs. Forrester died, back when she was twelve. She was too young to understand the loss of her grandparents. "I'm sorry, Will. Do you remember him at all?"

His expression was wistful, not full of pain. "Some blurry images. I'm not even sure if they're memories I hold, or if it's my mind's eye filling in pictures of the stories my mom has told me."

Jenna bit her lip, not sure how to proceed. His dad didn't look sick or old. Will stepped next to her and put his arm out for her to hug him. He tipped his head to the side and she did the same, both still looking at the picture. After a moment, he used the back of his hand to brush away some dust that had accumulated on the glass.

"Jenna, it's okay. I miss him, miss the idea of having a dad, but it was a long time ago. It's harder on my mom, of course, especially in June. The beginning of the month was their anniversary, and the end was when he died. He didn't feel well and stayed home from work. His heart stopped. It wasn't something that could have been detected or prevented." The "v" of a frown between his eyes cleared. "I like to think he's with us all the time, watching over us."

A lump had formed in the back of Jenna's throat thinking of Will without a dad to play catch, or to sit him down to talk about girls. She didn't trust herself to speak, so she just nodded, taking a step away from the mantle and turning her attention to the art on the connecting wall. It was a charcoal etching of a young boy of about two, holding a small ball. Jenna walked closer and began to smile. "Is this...?"

"Yes, it's me. Mom is very talented. She's done some other drawings throughout the house. At least the ones she's deemed good enough to frame. Although, I believe everything she either paints or draws is quite good."

From that wall in the corner was a television, on the opposite corner a huge Ficus plant. Not far from that was a metal stand full of movies. A sideboard table full of magazines and more knick-knacks completed that wall. Two plump couches were placed horizontally in the room. Across from the fireplace was a recessed bookshelf. A door led them into a small bathroom. It was monochromatic in black and white with red accent pieces and had a French flair to it. Even the sink was a retro design. There was a second door across from the first that opened back up into the red room.

"I'm going to get lost in here for sure," Jenna confessed.

"No, you won't," Will answered confidently. "It won't take you long at all to figure it out. It goes around in a circle. See?" He brought her back onto the other side of the red room and back into the tv room to an unobtrusive doorway Jenna hadn't seen at first. It abruptly turned into a winding staircase that led up to the next level.

"Are these part of the same stairs by the front door?"

"No, it's a different set. One on each end of the house."

These appeared to be nearly vertical. It reminded Jenna of the museum. Stairs in old buildings were very dangerous, too steep with narrow footing. One misstep would be all it would take to get killed, she thought. Will seemed to be following her thoughts as he usually did.

"The stairs are a bit tricky. They remind me of the bleachers in Yankee Stadium. Up we go."

Jenna was surprised. "You've been to Yankee Stadium?"

"Just once. New York City is not the best environment for someone like me," he admitted, turning around to wink at her.

"Oh, because you're a super empath? I thought you said you were able to block out the emotions of others."

Will kept his attention to what was in front of him to hide his blush. "I wouldn't say I'm a super empath. Yes, I use walls, but it's a lot of work with that many people, especially those who are passionate about sports and the arts." When Jenna agreed, he continued. "You've been there too?"

"Only one time," Jenna answered. "Dad won a raffle at work last April and took me and Pete. I don't even remember who the Yankee's played, I was too focused on trying to stay warm. And also hoping the guy who kept making beer runs wouldn't tumble all the way down to first base."

Will came out onto the landing first and turned to wait, his grin never fading. Looking around her, Jenna decided it was unsafe for sure. The staircase was just a huge hole in the floor—no railings, no lengthy area to prepare you for a change in levels.

"Like we said, still a lot to do." Will advanced slowly down the long hallway, pointing out extra rooms they weren't yet using. When Will stopped, Jenna noted four doors clustered close to each other.

"We call this area the quad." He opened the first door on the left which was a bathroom. It was done in a silver, turquoise, and brown combination that had the feel of the nineteen twenties. As soon as the light went on Jenna giggled.

"What?" Will asked.

"Your bathroom is done in our school colors."

"Well, we didn't know brown and blue were the school

colors until after we had the color schemes picked out. It is kinda funny, though. Rah, rah."

"Go team, go. Get it?" Jenna laughed.

Will slid his arm around her shoulders as he turned the light back off. "You're a goof."

They continued down the hallway, to two doors on the right that were his and Sulis's bedrooms. They were regular bedrooms, not macabre in the slightest. Will's room was done simply in different tones of blue that blended well with his oak furniture. It opened facing a window with denim-like shades, and to the left was his bed across from a large closet with a full-length mirror. It smelled good in there, a fruity-woodsy smell that was appealing to her. Except for the window being directly across from the doorway, Sulis's room was exactly the opposite of Will's, done in burgundy with gold accents.

"Mom did these, too."

More pictures were scattered on one wall. There was a grouping of three in matching frames. Each was of a girl done in what looked to Jenna like pastels. One was short in a cartoonish sort of way, wearing clothes befitting a nun. She had a Bible in her hands and a headpiece of a cross that hung down on her forehead. One was a blond girl in a prairie hat with long braids with pink ribbons at the end that matched her pink dress with white pinafore. She was carrying a bouquet of wildflowers that spilled over her hands. The last was a brunette wearing a renais-sance-style dress that had long, draping sleeves, and square-cut neckline. Her hair was held by a mesh headdress that matched the colors in her gown. She was carrying a thick book.

Another picture looked as if he had been on a piece of

stationary paper and was in a simple black frame. It was of a horse standing next to a cowgirl with a wide brimmed hat, freckles and exaggerated hips and bosom. The horse had his mouth open with all its teeth exposed as if laughing. The cowgirl's expression was one of embarrassment. Jenna started to read out loud the conversation bubbles over their heads only to stop midway, her hand coming up to her mouth to contain a snicker as her face started to redden.

"Yeah, well, Mom also has a wicked sense of humor," Will replied uncomfortably.

Jenna was beginning to wonder what she had really expected.

The last room was generously sized. It was clean but completely untouched, showing the true age of the house. The walls were in desperate need of paint, and the floors hadn't been buffed or waxed yet. It was a dreary contrast to the rest of their color pallet. Across from the doorway was Sulis's altar under the window. It had a black lace cloth with a spider web design over the top. It was neatly arranged with candle holders of all shapes and sizes with tapers in assorted colors. A regular, cup-sized goblet that looked like tarnished brass was off to one side. With a moment of confusion, Jenna recognized an incense burner and gasped.

"Oh, Will, this is beautiful!" she exclaimed as she pushed her hair back behind her shoulders and peered down to see the details. It was a piece of wood in the shape of a tall, jagged mountain, with a wolf sitting on top. His head was arched back in a howl towards the sky. Below him, the wood extended outward to accommodate the ashes of the incense in the shape of a narrow pond with what looked like the wolf's reflection in it.

"That has a cool story behind it. Mom had a vision during a meditation in one of our ceremonies about the wolf and wrote down what image she had seen. She thought it would make a great addition to our altar, to represent the Native American aspect of my father's family. She couldn't do wood carvings, so she went on a mission to find someone who could.

"My Aunt Mina had a retired neighbor who was into woodworking and lathing, and offered to try to do it. He went off the drawing blueprint Mom supplied, and it came out almost exactly as the picture. Made Mom tear up in front of me, something I rarely see. The price of it was amazingly small but paid off really well." Will looked at Jenna and smiled. "He wanted only thirty dollars and four of her readings."

"That's certainly modest," Jenna commented.

"So, she paid him and met with him one night each week for a month. The night before the fourth reading my mom had a dream about him. She told him she saw him play a specific game at the casino not too far away. She said he should go and play. Even the cards she read for him that night showed good fortune. He was hesitant, being on a fixed budget and all, but he went there, trusting her. He won the jackpot on his second spin. Fifty thousand dollars."

Two

*J*ENNA STOOD UP as her jaw dropped. "No way!"

Will nodded. "Yes, way. Now, whatever wood carvings we need, he'll do for us for free for the rest of our lives."

"That is so cool."

"It was the only time that's happened to her."

Jenna's gaze returned to the altar again, and within a few seconds, the frown returned. Almost in the shape of a Viking ship was a wooden bowl that was about two inches long. It held a teeny tiny wooden spoon.

"What is that for?"

"It's for holding salt. It's called a salt cellar."

"You lost me. I forgot what the salt is for," Jenna admitted.

"I wouldn't have expected you to remember it. What you've experienced us doing was a rushed affair, not a full ceremony, so it didn't have everything. You know how we always talk about energy? Well, before we work in a certain area, we need to make sure it's clean. We clean it physically as well as spiritually. Purifying is a way of spiritually cleaning a space of negative energy or even energy in excessive amounts. Salt does that."

Jenna was eager to learn more. "So, you need to use salt every time?"

"Not necessarily. You could also use stones. You just need to be careful to do your research to find which stones repel and which ones absorb negative energy. Sometimes a stone that will work for one person won't be as effective for another."

"You know a lot about stones and gems, too?"

"It helps."

"Huh." Jenna looked at all the random stones that were scattered about. She didn't know what any of them were. Their colors ranged from solids to swirls. Sulis's athame held a prominent place in the very middle. The burned design of flowery swirls on the leather sheath matched a lot of the designs in her home. The only part of the knife that was visible was the handle. It was bound with brown twine.

"So, everyone also needs an athame?" Jenna beamed a little at saying the name correctly for the first time.

"Good job! No, it's a matter of preference. We have athames because that's what we like to use. Some people use wands or staffs. Others prefer to just use their bare hands. This athame is mine."

Jenna bent down to the altar to see better, and this time, held her long hair back with both hands by her shoulders. The knife was encased in a simple, shiny leather that looked dark as if had been treated with waterproofing oil. The handle was also wood, carved with a round swirl and adorned with a single small red stone near the blade. Will reached down and took it out of its sheath. Its straight blade was curved, thicker in the middle, with a sharp point. The whole athame was about eight inches long.

"Tell me about this again," Jenna asked, pointing to a star within a circle.

Patiently, Will answered Jenna as he studied her. "That's a pentacle."

Jenna thought about the séance his mother had initiated with Tina and Toby and their fathers after Will accidentally lobbed an apple and broke the second story window in the museum. Both had to reveal they were Pagans—witches— and their talent would be instrumental in trying to close that stubborn portal.

Of course, nothing at 713 Sentinel was ever easy, and teenagers rarely made smart choices. Bad decisions like apple chucking aside, trouble arose that particular evening when Jenna and Will fell into an old photograph of the building recently discovered in Will's house. They were transported back in time a hundred and fifty years to when the museum was a boarding house, just as Amelie, the owner's daughter, was killed. That adventure resulted in ghosts crossing over into their present time. As things tended to circle around for Jenna, she easily becoming the medium for Amelie, just as she had been the vessel for Elizabeth Avery back when the museum was a mill a hundred years after that timeframe.

Will and Jenna had also learned from their experience that those bad guys had buried large and valuable Herkimer diamonds somewhere on the property. That led to mistake number two: keeping that knowledge to themselves while they dug for it on their own. Keeping secrets always has a price, and Jenna almost lost Will in betraying his trust when she told the others.

The group learned that Sylvia, Amelie's mother, was a powerful white witch herself, capable of spell work that actively spanned decades. Between Will, his mother, and Jenna's group, they finally sealed the window. The first was when Will drove Sylvia's athame into the double hung, then second was during Sylvia's spell which carried and coated the lock with wax from a unique turquoise candle.

Jenna's face turned a little pink. "So, it's really not like a sign of the devil or anything? That stuff that happened at the museum…"

"Ah," said Will, understanding her trepidation. He shook his head with a slight grin. "No, it has nothing to do with demonic worshipping. In fact, most Wiccans don't believe in hell or the devil." Jenna's eyebrows shot up and disappeared under her thick bangs. Will was quick to continue. "What we've encountered at the museum may well change our minds about that." He thought a moment. "Hmm, no, they were people who were evil. Not the same."

"Oh. What does that star stand for, then?" Jenna gingerly touched the wooden disk.

"The star is called a pentagram. The symbol itself has roots dating back as early as 3000 BC, and has been used by many cultures and religions. Even Christianity used it as one time where each point represented the five wounds of Jesus.

In Paganism, a circle around the star protects the pentagram which is then called a pentacle. For us, a pentacle with five points represent the elements."

Jenna was quiet, thinking. "But there are only four directions: east, west, north, and south."

"You are so quick," Will said before flashing his crooked smile. He reached down to trace her fingers with his own. When he spoke again, it was barely a whisper. "You didn't include spirit. It's the top point."

She stared at his hand over hers and looked up, not realizing how close he was to her. "What exactly is spirit?" she managed to articulate.

"Spirit connects everything together. The other four are tangible, physical. Spirit is the divine in us and the link to our spiritual well. It binds our feet on the ground with magic and our Gods and Goddesses that surround us. Some cultures identify spirit as love."

"That's beautiful." Not backing away, she studied his face slowly, her eyes taking in every nuance. She liked what she saw. His face was patient, honest, and handsome. She found her eyes resting on his lips. It felt as if the oxygen in the room had vanished. Jenna breathed deeply to calm her heart only for her nose to be filled with the woodsy and citrus fragrance that was purely Will. Before she knew it, she was leaning into him, the butterflies in her stomach frantic, as her lips kissed his. Instead of setting the butterflies free, it made them more frenzied, and her breath came quicker. Will's fingers laced into hers, and her free hand found its way to his face and around his neck.

Will kissed her just as intently and after a moment, his

hand was on her arm, pulling away. He squeezed her hand gently and looked back at the altar. "We use the pentacle to either ground or charge objects."

Jenna nodded silently as she collected herself, and turned her attention to a stout glass curio cabinet. Figurines of small dragons, gnomes, and faeries with elongated ears and feet were placed neatly by clear crystals that looked like small swords. A small statue of a black panther was set next to one of an owl. A piece of clay art—of five women making a circle by holding hands—surrounded a tall weeping willow tree, filled the glass shelf.

"This will be our room for ceremony once we're finished," Will said, putting his hands in his pockets. Jenna's eyes grew wide with curiosity. "You know how we had a circle on Halloween last month? When we were able to join Amelie and her mother, and finish the spell to put Jonas and Henry away for good? It's like that. We try to have a permanent space, a sacred space. The longer you use a specific place, the more energy is stored there to be used. After the kitchen is done, this room is next."

"I remember you using my wrist to draw the eight sabbats, or ceremonies, you have."

"Yup. They happen to coincide with the holidays Christians celebrate. Some are the same. Well, most started with us, but I won't go into that right now. Anyway, all that stuff at the museum kind of overshadowed our biggest holiday, Samhain, which is known as Halloween to everyone else."

"Sow-what? What's the name? You told me about the reason for the ceremonies, but not their names."

"I guess I didn't want to overload you. They're tough, I

know. You should try spelling them. This one has several pronunciations. We say *sow*-in, not anything like its phonetical pronunciation. The next one is easy. Yule is on December twenty-first." Will thought a moment. "Hmm, maybe you can join us. It gets pretty loud beforehand, like a party. My aunts join us. It would be fun. You could meet the rest of my family."

"Really?" asked Jenna excitedly before her brow furrowed. She worried she would be intruding. The things that were done in the museum were what Sulis had offered. She wondered if this would be too personal. "Would they mind? I don't want to make anyone feel uncomfortable with me tagging along."

They walked a few steps to a small bench in the long hallway and sat down.

"I doubt they would. I'm sure of it, but I'll run it by Mom just to make sure. Maybe you can come to our Full Moon Ceremony first to see if you'll like it. That one will be at the end of first week of December." Will hesitated on the last words, his grin faltering.

"Then why do you look nervous? I'm not scared of your ceremonies," Jenna murmured.

Will laughed a bit uncomfortably. "You haven't met my family yet."

Jenna's face fell. "Why? What about them?"

A sly smile crossed Will's face. "Nothing I haven't told you about. But you haven't met them yet. They're likely to speak their minds, and I'm sure I have supplied them with enough fodder in my short and entertaining life. Between the five of them, my mom was the only one to have kids. So, in a way, I'm looked upon as an only child to each of them. There's nothing to distract them from asking what goes on in my life. And since my mother is close to her sisters, they sometimes get every last detail. Probably all of them. I don't mind, though, they're good people. I'm just nervous they'll embarrass me beyond my ability to repair my image."

"How is it none of them had a family?

"Aunt Diane didn't have the best first marriage and she was much older when she remarried. She's a widower now like Aunt Mina. Aunt Lee preferred animals to babies, and Aunt Whitty never married."

"Oh, I'm sorry they lost their husbands," Jenna offered.

Will shrugged. "They were too for a while, but they're not bitter about it. They grieved and moved on, like mom has. They seem to like the freedom of being their own person, considering that generation put a lot of stock into having a man to be happy."

"So, they're progressive?"

Will tipped his head back and laughed outright. "That can't be more accurate, Jenna."

Jenna relaxed as her smile returned. She started to get up when something rubbed against her leg. She jumped, startled.

"Hey there, Rommy." Will bent down and scooped up a short-haired cat that meowed as if in response. He was mostly black except for grey in his face, one paw, and the tip of his tail. The black on his head looked a lot like a hairline, complete with the color extending down the bridge of his nose. The cat leaned toward Jenna, waiting to be petted. Jenna ruffled up his fur as he started to purr loudly.

"Not Zeus, huh? That would have made sense."

"Yeah, well, we're fans of Star Trek, and it kind of rubs off on you," replied Will. He quickly kissed Jenna on the cheek, and she blushed in spite of herself.

"So, what part of the house will you impress me with next?"

Will looked up to the ceiling briefly. We only have the very high and the very low levels. The attic isn't remarkable but the basement sure is. Do you want to do that? You can see the attic after dinner?"

"I'm game."

Will led her down another staircase and Jenna found herself by the front door. They following the delicious aromas into the kitchen to another set of stairs that led into the basement.

"The pasta just went in, Will. Don't take too long."

"Okay. We'll take a quick tour of downstairs."

"Be careful coming back up."

"Are you sure you don't need help with anything?" Jenna offered, turning to Sulis while Will retrieved a flashlight.

"Thank you, but no, everything is under control," Sulis answered with a wink.

Will motioned for Jenna as he clicked the light switch on the wall. They stopped at the ancient basement door, his hand on the handle before the door swung away from them. "This is another thing on our list to fix. We're not sure why anyone would have put in a door that opens out to a stairway, but here it is. It makes it especially awkward to open once you're down there."

The steps to the basement were steep as well and took them into the middle of the basement. Two drop-down lightbulbs, one way to the left and one in the very back, did little to lighten the space. The basement stretched the length of the house and was built with courses of large stones, the same way the museum was. A random thought of how hard it must have been to build a house without cement crossed Jenna's mind. This was familiar to her. It always reminded her of large cobblestones. On the right wall, underneath a small window, was a large cistern about twelve feet long. It looked about the same size as her family's old blow-up pool from a few years ago. Even though Jenna knew what a cistern was, she let Will explain. She enjoyed how proud and energetic he was about something so old.

"This is our cistern which is for holding harvested water. Rainwater could be collected by a rain barrel, and then gravity would take it down here into this indoor, waterproofed tank, to be stored. That water supplied the whole house's needs. We haven't tested it yet to see if it'll still hold water without leaking. We'd like to try to find a use for ours once the house is finished. Not to drink, of course, but we could maybe use it for laundry or something. Come here and see this."

Jenna looked around her as she followed Will. Across from the stairs, almost in the middle of the room, was a whole area filled with plastic totes and large cardboard boxes. Their final destination written in marker on their sides.

"Once the rest of the rooms are completed, we can finally unpack everything. The kitchen is bare bones right now with just the basics, so a lot is still boxed. The same with our spare bedroom." Will led her around to the back corner and took a rusty skeleton key off an ancient peg on the wall.

"Here's our canning cellar."

The key clicked loudly in the lock in the silent room, and Will had to push the door open with some effort. He turned on the flashlight and turned it upward, dimly illuminating the small room which was a little bigger than the size of a garden shed.

"Don't you have electricity in here?"

"Illumination for this whole level is subpar. The former owners didn't feel it necessary to invest in anything more than required, and the canning cellar wasn't wired. Apparently, it was never used. So, no light in here yet except for what comes through that postage stamp-sized window."

"Shoot. Uh, oh. I must have grabbed the old flashlight by mistake. These batteries are on their way out," Will muttered, as the flashlight beam weakened. "Anyway, general stores, back in the day, were for basic items like salt, sugar, coffee, and flour. People were self-sufficient and had to supply their own food. They would raise their own livestock and have a crop. After harvest, they would smoke the meats and can the vegetables to use throughout the winter when it was too cold to grow anything."

Now it was Jenna's turn to smile. "What do you know about canning?" she baited.

"Hmm," Will answered, his eyes twinkling in the dim light as he picked up the challenge. "Food was either raw packed, or blanched and hot packed, depending on the food. Then it was put in canning jars with syrup or brine, and sealed. Using high temperatures of boiling water, the jars would be submerged. The heat would create a vacuum seal on the tops by pulling all the air out. That way the jars could be stored unrefrigerated.

And," he said, pointing his finger to draw out the moment, "the canning cellar was a pantry room with a stable temperature where all the canned food was kept until it was used." His hands indicated the small room in a Vanna White sort of way. "Considering canned foods had a very long shelf life, this type of room would be necessary to hold it all. It was always in the basement where it's a little cooler, and dark, and generally not disturbed. Canning cellars might hold jars of jams, chutneys, sauces, pickles, fruits, veggies, and even meats. Even a bin of potatoes or onions could be kept here." You probably know all about this, though, huh?" he asked, his excitement fading.

"Almost, but your knowledge is impressive, and I enjoy your enthusiasm. Not many people get excited about antiques or things like this," Jenna admitted, watching how his face glowed with pride. She looked around.

The built-in shelves against the far wall were dirty but bare. Will walked in further, the beam of light momentarily brightening, as it shown down to an inset little cubby area in the right corner that was just big enough to stand in. It was made from courses of stones like the entire basement, and circled around on itself. Jenna immediately thought of the photography dark room at school, or of a winding entranceway into a public bathroom. Oddly, it didn't lead anywhere. The micro hallway ended abruptly in a flat slab of wood. It looked like it had been cut from a huge tree. It was rustic, with rough bark and stubs where small branches had grown. It was very much abused with gouges. There were scratches and what appeared to be elongated burn marks over its length as well as several large holes that sat vacantly where weak knots had once been.

"The floor in here is where we found all the pictures of the boarding house."

"I can see why no one else had found them until now. That's a cool hiding place. How did you come across them?" Jenna asked.

"I'm really not sure. We weren't looking for anything in particular, just snooping around and tallying all the work we had ahead of us. I guess I felt the need to look in the corner. I'm thin enough to squeeze in."

"Why is there a wedge of tree in here? What is that board for?" Jenna wondered. She took the flashlight to get a better look. She fit easily in the nook but the light had diminished further. It was still too dark to see the board clearly. The markings she could see looked like hieroglyphics.

Will wedged himself next to Jenna. She was distracted enough by their closeness to forget why she was there in the first place. Her breathing sped up, and his cologne filled her nose, making her thoughts drift and mesh with signals from her body she was unfamiliar with. Her face became hot as if she was blushing, and she felt sweaty. The urge to wrap her arms around Will to kiss him again was overwhelming. She was dumbfounded and confused, unable to focus her attention on the question she had asked. She stood there motionless. Will excused himself quietly and backed out.

"We don't know what the board is for. There are some symbols on it that are pretty cool, though. What do you think when you look at the sides? I couldn't really tell if it was marked up before it was put in or after," Will questioned, his voice now husky. If he had felt anything next to Jenna, he didn't mention it. He cleared his throat, his voice sounding more like his own. "I tried to do some research on its purpose. It's something I've never seen in all the historical books I've looked into. I couldn't even find anything remotely close online."

"I can't tell either," Jenna answered walking back into the center of the canning room. "Did you ever find out why those pictures were here? I got the feeling that Sylvia had only lived in the boarding house. Why would so many pictures of that building be buried here in this basement?"

"We wondered, too, but haven't found anything out. All we could find were the names of the house's owners all the way to 1869, but nothing jumped out at us. Not much else would be listed in the town hall records. Maybe there was a connection to the person who built it?" Will offered, shrugging. He smiled again easily. "Dinner's got to be ready. Let's go."

Three

THE SPAGHETTI AND homemade sauce Sulis made, along with the fresh Italian bread and salad was wonderful. Jenna laughed at the lighthearted banter and digging between Will and his mom. Now that they weren't in imminent danger at the museum, they were able to really get to know one another. Jenna realized not only was Sulis incredibly smart, she was actually very funny.

"...and that's why Will won't ever have another pet rabbit," Sulis finished. Jenna laughed at the story and Will shrugged, unable to dispute the tale.

"So, Jenna. What are your hobbies? What do you like to do?"

Jenna finished chewing a cucumber. "Other than reading? I like to sing. I was in chorus in middle school, and now I'm in the high school choir and Chamber Singers. That's a small group by audition only, unlike the choir which is open to all high schoolers. We do some secular music, but mostly it's sacred. Both are at a higher degree of difficulty and I like the challenge. Kinda like this." Jenna tilted her head to the room adjacent to the kitchen where the stereo played a classical Irish song.

"That's very impressive. Which section are you in?"

"Thank you. I've been both soprano and alto. The first two years Mrs. Howland wanted me to concentrate on my upper range. The last two years I've been working on my lower register, so I'm an alto. It's how I would describe myself. We have concerts with a few special events. Fall into winter are our busiest months. We have a caroling night, and also go to the retirement home up past the mall. I love to see the seniors' faces light up when we sing, but I also like sitting and talking with them. They must be lonely because they just go on and on. It's exhausting, though. Sometimes I go home happy, but mostly I go home either completely bummed or really tired. I don't know if it's because it's the last event we have or what, but it takes me a day or two to recover."

"I don't doubt it at all," Sulis replied as she put down her glass of lemon water. "I wondered about that. So, you are an empath as well as a sensitive. That's not surprising." Will's eyes widened as if he didn't think of it but should have.

"What do you mean? I'm a what?"

"You are a sensitive; you're more aware of your environment than those around you. Being an empath is being open to taking on an experience of another."

"I'm not an empath like Will, though. I can't project moods onto people," Jenna admitted.

"No, Will's gifts go beyond most people's abilities, but there are a lot of empaths out there. Not all of them are sensitives," Sulis explained. "Tell me, do you like being in big crowds? Do you go to concerts or the State Fair?"

Jenna thought about it as she twirled a forkful of pasta. "I've gone, but I don't seem to enjoy it much as everyone else does. I guess I get too wound up. No one else looks as overloaded as I feel."

Sulis nodded in understanding. "What about Homecoming?"

The fork stopped in mid-air as she took a moment to think it over. Will finished wiping his mouth and ran his hand through his hair. "We went together. I thought you enjoyed yourself?"

"Oh no, Will, I did have a good time! This year was different." She grabbed his hand and squeezed it to show she meant it, then frowned, confused. "Being there wasn't as bad as it usually is."

Will kissed her hand before helping himself to another spoonful of pasta. Jenna shook her head politely when he offered her seconds.

Sulis had continued nodding. "That makes sense. I bet you were focusing on Will and ignoring everything else."

The blush that crept across Jenna's face confirmed as much. Sulis's lips turned up, amused. "Your attention to Will served as a barrier, and I bet you didn't even realize it. That doesn't come as easily. You need to purposely learn to shield. That's why you leave the old folks' home so tired. You attract spirits in the museum and connect with others through their dreams because, as a sensitive, you're so open to everything. I picked that up from you the day we bumped into each other in the store.

"There's something about being an empath that allows people to open up and tell you things they wouldn't normally tell a stranger. They feel safe around you. The problem is they tend to dump out their problems and worries without even thinking about it, and you absorb them by directly experiencing what they are feeling. That can be their physical ailments, emotions, or mental struggles. It's not exactly safe and—as you've learned—draining."

Jenna had almost forgotten about the food in her mouth and had to close her jaw to maintain her table manners. She took a moment to process the information as she used her napkin. "Wow. I didn't know. Where can I go to learn shielding?"

"We can talk about it another time. I can help you."

"So, do you do things like that for a living?"

Will snorted and crumbs from the bread he was biting into scattered on his plate. His mother gave him a disapproving look. "No, we do those things on our own. I'm a marketing director."

"Oh. I guess I thought you went to school for all this creativity." She indicated the house with one hand while she crossed her knife and fork on her plate, sitting back in her chair.

Sulis laughed as surprise colored Jenna's face. "I did. I went to Boston for fine art. Actually, that was where I met Will's father. There are a lot of different classes in the curriculum; design, painting, drawing, color, concept. I tried to turn the degree into one with the most employment stability. I'm pretty versatile. There were seven of us in my family, and we didn't have much when we were growing up. A lot of things were hand-me-downs or from second hand stores, so we had to be innovative and creative. I had some raw talent, and I'm very sure the mind frame of looking at objects differently helped."

"I'll say. Your artwork is beautiful."

"Thank you. It's a huge part of my life, but I was never destined to be a starving artist. Well, other than the time I dressed as one for Halloween."

"Halloween has always been my favorite holiday. I've almost always gone as a witch," Jenna admitted without thinking, taking a stack of dirty plates to the sink. For a heartbeat she thought she might have offended them both. "Oh, I didn't mean…"

Will was right behind her with the serving and salad bowls. "That's actually kind of funny."

"Please, Jenna, you should know us better by now. No offense taken. A witch, huh?" Sulis asked, raising one eyebrow. There was a sparkle in her eye as if she found it comical, but not at all surprising.

"Yeah, that phase lasted forever. Every year for something like, six Halloweens. It drove my mom crazy because I honestly didn't want to be anything else. But it wasn't just the holiday, though. I couldn't get enough about witches or witchcraft in general. I took out just about every book the school library had, and quite a few from the public one. That was back when I was living in Steele City. Oh, here's the stinky cheese."

"Thank you," Sulis answered, taking the Parmesan from

her, and reaching for the butter on the counter. "So, when did the obsession stop?"

"After the first year we moved here, I think. Probably when I started to spend more time at the old mill." Jenna didn't make the connection the other two did as her thoughts went in another direction. "I used to write my own spells on index cards and make my own potions." Her gaze shifted inward thinking back to her childhood. "If anything, I made some nice smelling potpourri."

Will had stopped what he was doing, and Sulis turned towards Jenna, the refrigerator door wide open. "What did you make them with?" There was almost an anticipation in the way she asked. Jenna took the dish cloth, her attention on wiping the table.

"Oh, poplar leaves I'd crush up with a sharp stone, bark from an oak tree, and berries. Then I'd raid the kitchen and add bay leaves, cinnamon sticks or hibiscus and chamomile leaves from a tea bag." She giggled. "Tina used to call it "camel meal" all the time. She never really liked to do that sort of stuff, but she'd watch me. That is, when she could actually see anything. She had these plastic barrettes that always held like, 10 strands of hair. Most ended up hanging in front her face."

"What made you add those sorts of things?"

Jenna shrugged as she gathered the loose crumbs in her hand, still oblivious to the interest this generated. "I don't know, why?" She looked up and realized both were watching her. Will was leaning against the counter with the strangest expression on his face. Sulis was looking at her intently, the fridge door still open wide. Something humorous passed in her eyes, and she shook her head as if dismissing the thought. "No reason."

"What am I missing?" Jenna asked, feeling left out.

"Nothing," Will answered, before adding, "I can only imagine Tina with messy hair. There's no way she'd be seen like that today."

"Miss Put Together. I know, right?"

"Speaking of being aware of one's appearance, did you know Will is a Trekkie and once went trick-or-treating as a Starfleet Commander?"

Will flushed, but was unfazed, his eyes alight with playfulness. He tapped his fingers on the counter in rhythm to the music from the other room. "There's worse things than a Starfleet Commander."

"That's for sure," Jenna agreed. She knew there was more they weren't saying, but left it alone. "I dressed up to attend a Trek convention in the city a few years ago. There was a group of guys loaded into a pickup truck who were dressed up as Ferengi. They stuck out so much the police officer doing traffic control pulled them over for an expired inspection."

Will had been staring at Jenna, his head cocked to the side, his gaze completely one of awe. "You went to a Trek convention?" It seemed to take him a second for his head to wrap around the idea. Jenna could almost read the thoughts in his head with the way his expressions morphed: surprise, reverence, and something that looked a lot like passion before it settled on adoration. "Who'd you dress as?"

"Deanna Troy."

"Very apropos," Sulis said, her back now to them, filling the sink with sudsy water.

"Anyway, that was the year I bought mom a Yule gift of a year's worth of therapy to hypnotize her to stay away from public auctions. Oh, that reminds me. I thought Jenna might like to come to the Full Moon Ceremony. Is that okay by you?"

"I think that's a nice idea!" Sulis exclaimed, turning and wiping her hands on the dish towel. "Celebrating is so much better than what you've experienced us doing. Different, too. Ceremony is the evening of December second. Yule is only a few weeks after that, if you'd like to join us."

"I'd love to, thank you."

"I've got these tonight, Will. Why don't you go get some games from the other room?" When he nodded, Sulis returned to the dishes, the air swirling with steam, making the window in front of her start to fog.

"You are completely amazing!" Will admitted, once they left the kitchen. He picked Jenna up and twirled her around once as she let out a squeal. He kissed her on her forehead but didn't let her out of his arms. "Never in a million years would I have imagined being lucky enough to find someone who not only deals with the magical realm, but who doesn't look down on sci fi shows. If only you can handle our ceremonies." His expression turned to mock seriousness. "It's not the spirits you have to worry about. Like I said, it's my family. Just like tonight, you've been getting it in small doses with my mom. It gets much worse."

Jenna kissed Will on the cheek as he released her into a twirl. She held herself confidently and adjusted her shirt again.

"That's okay, I'm up for it." She watched Will bend down to the shelf where the games were stacked and blew her bangs out from her eyes. "Hey, Will? Why the interest in my pseudo-witch concoctions?"

Yahtzee was near the bottom but snagged on something. Will leaned in closer to shimmy the box, his voice a bit muffled. "Huh? Oh, well, your potions ingredients weren't too far off from what some spells call for. You truly are a natural."

"Hmm."

With the speakers temporarily hooked up into the kitchen, the turntable chose from five different CD's while they played a few dice games. Everyone was about the same in winnings until they played Scrabble. Sulis beat the socks off everyone. Jenna was unsure how anyone could ever remember all the words Sulis had a working knowledge of. Laughter filled the room often and loudly. Tonal music with a soprano lilting in the background gave the evening a distinctive, removed quality. Jenna enjoyed the evening immensely, especially the quirky sense of humor Sulis had.

Jenna rubbed her face from smiling. "You both are too much. My stomach muscles hurt from laughing so hard." She looked up at the clock on the wall and did a double take. "Is it really after nine already? My curfew is ten. Let me help clean up."

Sulis started to replace the game tiles in the box. "Thank you, but I can get these on my own in a few minutes. It's been a pleasure, Jenna. You are welcome here any time."

"It's a beautiful house, too. The work you've done is incredible."

Will frowned. "Oh, we never did make it to the attic."

"Would you mind, Jenna? There's not much to it but I'd appreciate your thoughts on the windows up there. The panes have a soft blue hue and look like antique glass to me, but I'm no expert."

"Sure, I'd be happy to check it out." Jenna's attention shifted to the cat who stood just out of reach. As Jenna followed Rommy, Sulis started for the bathroom, stopping briefly to tap Will on his shoulder. "Don't forget of the flashlights from the kitchen drawer."

"Okay."

Jenna returned, holding the purring ball of fur. She kissed his head. "He's a snuggler, isn't he?"

Will smiled as they walked around into the tv room. "I would have said he's my cat until just now seeing how he lets you hold him. Cats are funny. When we watch television, he makes it obvious he's in charge of who he visits." Rommy jumped out of her arms. "See? What did I tell you? Cats are funny, come on."

They went up the oddly set stairs in the side of the wall. These wound around to an attic-like room. It was thick and musty. Will fumbled for a switch, and the light brightened slowly. It was definitely an attic: chilly and empty, except for a few odds and ends covered with several inches of dirt.

"These things aren't ours. We still have to clean this out, but there's loads of room up here." Will coughed and rubbed his eyes as the dust was kicked up. "It's still pretty cool. It is almost like another living space; it's high enough, and there are partitions that separate into different rooms. I'm not sure why you would need to have more living space with the size of this house and not use it for storage instead. Right over there are the two tiny windows mom was talking about."

Jenna had gone on ahead alone. Brittle crackling under her feet from the floorboards made her tread lightly. She touched the walls, intrigued by the difference in bare wood studs and lack of insulation like newer homes. The dimensions of today's carpentry clearly showed how quickly framework could be put up with precision. These wood planks were slender, some with variances in size. Each rusted nail was driven in with hard work and effort, not a nail gun. Jenna walked the length of the room, her hands delicately caressing the craftsmanship.

"Hey, don't go too far, Jenna. We haven't explored much up here," Will began, lurching toward her. Jenna turned around to dramatically lean against the wall to show she wasn't worried, just as Will reached out to her. He tripped over the last step, his boot getting stuck in a raised floorboard, his momentum carrying his weight into her, pushing her through the weak partition. She had no time or way to adjust her stance, and fell backwards, squinting her eyes shut as if they could brace her fall.

Four

*S*HE LANDED HARD on her back on the wood, her head hitting solidly. It knocked the wind out of her. She lay there, gasping loudly, trying to draw her breath in around the invisible rock she felt in her chest. The need to get oxygen ruled out all other thoughts as she looked ahead seeing nothing. Her vision swam in front of her before it focused on the shape of a face; a haggard man's face. The eyes were pulled down in anger, and the cheeks, speckled with stubble, sagged almost like there were no teeth inside to hold the proper shape. The thin lips were set firmly in a scowl.

She drew in another ragged breath, unaware of Will yelling near her ear. The face became clear just for a moment before the stars and flashes of light occluded the details and disappeared. Jenna's eyes slowly focused, and Will's face appeared, his anxious voice coming to her as if the volume was being turned on from mute.

"… something, Jenna! Can you breathe okay?" he asked, panicked. He turned around, speaking behind him, and when he looked back at Jenna, he relaxed a bit. Her eyes were now tracking him, and her breathing was evening out.

"I feel so stupid. I got the wind knocked out of me," Jenna managed to force out. She sat up slowly and closed her eyes in embarrassment.

"It's okay, she's okay!" Will hollered towards the doorway, helping Jenna sit up.

"Are you sure? What happened?" Sulis's voice floated up from downstairs.

"We fell through one of the interior walls. There's another area up here!" Will yelled. He scrambled around Jenna now, and judged the stability of the remaining wall that surrounded the damage. When it seemed secure enough, he poked his head into the black hole.

"Ugh. I forgot the flashlight and it's too dark to see anything! Good thing Mom showed up with another one. Plus, I was starting to panic. You're sure you're okay now?"

"Yeah," Jenna answered hoarsely, nodding, as she righted herself. She brushed off her shirt and bottom with her hands. A powdery dust floated up around her.

Will's attention went back to the hole, and when he turned again towards Jenna at the sound of his mother's voice from below, the start of a smirk played at the corners of his mouth. Jenna knew that look; it was one of mischief and intrigue.

"We're not sure it's safe up there, Will. Take a quick look and come right back down." Sulis's voice suddenly became clear as she popped her head through the door.

"Here's the flashlight. Catch!"

Will walked half the distance to his mother; his clunking boots the only sound. The dust was still swirling in the glow of the bulb above. He caught the light midway.

"We weren't told about this room from the previous owner. Then again, he lives in Florida now. Still, don't you think someone would know about it?" Will rambled excitedly as he went back to the hole. He rubbed Jenna's shoulder quickly before he clicked the light on and bent down.

Jenna, standing there awkwardly, sat back down on the floor and turned to look behind her. She sneezed twice, the man's face replaying oddly in her head when she closed her eyes. She wasn't sure what that was all about. The image was not familiar, definitely no one she recognized. It made her uncomfortable. The expression on his face was leering and devious.

"Huh. Check this out! There's an old water basin and some old blankets laid out like a bed," Will described.

Jenna was puzzled. "Why would there be a bedroom way up here?" Her thoughts again jumped to the haggard man's profile.

"Dunno," Will admitted, walking out into the main attic. He looked down at Jenna, stopped and frowned, really taking her in this time. "Are you okay?"

"Yeah," Jenna said slowly. "It's just that I saw a man's face when I was trying to catch my breath, and it's kinda staying with me."

Will's frown hadn't changed. He tentatively looked around him. "You saw a man here?"

"No," Jenna answered quickly, shaking her head, her hair

swishing side to side. "Just an image of one when my vision was all funny. Not of anyone actually here." Will sat down next to her, face to face. Concerned, he looked back and forth into her eyes.

"My head is fine."

"Uh huh." Will didn't sound convinced. "Maybe my mom can figure it out."

Jenna bowed her head, running her hands over her heated cheeks. "No, please don't, I'm mortified enough. It's nothing, I'm sure. And I've got to get home. My parents cut my curfew for a month as punishment from keeping the diamonds a secret around Halloween. I can't come home late."

He waited, torn with wanting to help, but also wanting to honor her wishes. "If you're sure." She nodded her head emphatically.

"Okay. If you say so."

Jenna still had concerns and questions about the man's image once she got in her car for the short ride home. She still felt she did the right thing by not saying anything to Sulis. The image of the man's face came back to Jenna each time she tried to concentrate on a different aspect of the evening. It was as if everything was linked to the stranger.

She questioned why the photos had been in their basement but couldn't piece together anything from the old boarding house. Who was the man she saw? Was he the owner? Why had she seen him? What did it mean? Shaking her head, she noted how excited Will seemed at the discovery of another room, but she wasn't. Instead, it made her uneasy? Why would four walls, some linen and a sink do that? The unease she felt circled back to the man, the features of his face resurfacing in her mind's eye.

Willing the restlessness of those thoughts away, she tried to figure out what the cubby was all about but couldn't go any further without her heartrate picking up. That train ran in several directions leaving her feeling scattered. She had to smile with the thought of how the tight space and Will's cologne made her feel. No one else had ever affected her that way before. Unfortunately, the smile faded almost as quickly as her mind returned to the unknown face. She certainly didn't understand the man's face either, just that idea had her very nervous.

The clock in the kitchen, visible through the glass in the front door by the stove's nightlight, said nine fifty-two. She entered quietly in case someone had gone to bed early, startling her dad sneaking ice cream.

"Oh," was the only thing he was able to say with his mouth full. He tried to quickly swallow the cold treat.

"You are so bad," Jenna scolded, locking the door behind her. He started to say something before grabbing his forehead. Jenna giggled. "I hope the brain freeze was worth it."

"Anything but getting caught by your mother is worth it," he said after recovering. "I'm glad you made it home on time. How was dinner?"

"Dinner was great. You know how you've been wondering what they've been doing inside? They are brilliant DIYers. Still a lot of work to go, but what they've done is amazing. Sulis should take up interior decorating."

Jenna shrugged out of her coat and hung it on the hook by the door. For a moment, she thought she'd just say goodnight and go to her room. They were alone and she really needed to talk this over. Confiding in him was easier than with her mother, it always had been, especially when it came to things like this. It made her feel better to get it off her chest, although it did nothing to diminish her discomfort.

"I'm glad you didn't really hurt yourself," her father replied after she stopped talking. "Sounds like something your mind must have dredged up from lack of air. That's happened to me before when I was young and stupid and owned a dirt bike, and it turned out to be nothing. Maybe it was just a trick of the lights. The rest of the night went okay, right? I wouldn't worry about it too much." He closed the package of chocolate chips and put it back in the pantry behind the bag of flour, kissed her quickly on the top of her head and went back to the television in the other room.

Jenna wasn't soothed. Holding her keys so they wouldn't make too much noise, she put them on the peg of the corkboard on the wall. She had explained it right. The spots she saw before she could get in enough air were random, not the same. She knew she saw a face. Or did she? Yawning, she tried to see her father's perspective. Maybe being a bit self-conscious about going to Will's house transferred into a scary person when her guard was down. Maybe she should stop psychoanalyzing herself. After climbing into bed, she fell asleep and dreamed about seemingly inconsequential things: sparkling gems used in a ceremony, Will, and an old country store from the Wild West.

THE NEXT DAY was Sunday, and Jenna had shopping to do. It was a rare, sunny day in November in Central New York. It was starting out as a mild winter with only a dusting of snow remaining from the two inches that had fallen the night before. She drove with the radio on, volume up high, singing along in harmony to Alicia Keys' melody in her strong, alto voice.

She rounded the corner past the museum on the way to the main road, concentrating on the song. She had a very good memory, each song categorized by where she was when she first heard it. She'd heard this song during summer vacation the year before. She smiled when she remembered how her brother had done an impersonation of the song in the car when they were on their way home from one of his many sports games. He had pretended his hockey stick was a piano. It was a very poor, but hilarious impression.

Jenna started to laugh, but it immediately choked off to a gasp. Stepping on the brakes, she stared, confused and scared. It wasn't quite noon yet, and the sun was not fully overhead. Shadows from the sun blocked by the lining trees crisscrossed naturally as the road bent and turned. In the middle of the clear, dry road in front of her was a wide stretch of sunshine with the man's face outlined by the shadows. Jenna blinked, wanting to erase the image as if she had forced herself to see it in the first place. It was still there, a snarl in his expression. She looked up at the oncoming traffic just in time to catch herself on the wrong side of the road. Swerving back to her own lane, she drew in a deep, shaky breath.

Turning down the radio, she drove more cautiously. Jenna thought about the face. She hadn't been thinking of anything particular that would have brought it up. Her thoughts immediately focused on her dreams. The Wild West wasn't a routine nighttime topic, but Will had been describing the history of his house and how people lived back when it was built. The gems could easily be explained as well. She decided she would call Tina later and chat. Her dad hadn't helped, and from the way Will acted in the attic when she told him what she saw, she decided not to broach the topic with him again so soon.

The rest of the day was uneventful, and as it wore on, she finally calmed down. No more faces snuck up on her. She called Tina after dinner.

"Well, I'm clueless, friend," Tina admitted.

"I just didn't like how Will watched me after I told him. I don't want him to think I obsess about ghosts. It's not like I need attention or anything."

"I'm sure he doesn't think that. Sorry to cut you off, but I need to retype my English essay for tomorrow. Dad found a whole bunch of little mistakes I need to fix. Keep me in the loop, though."

Jenna tried not to stress about the man's face. She was surprised but thankful she didn't have any odd dreams about it, and the next week started up as usual.

"AND THEN, THE older gentleman made a comment about the item I was holding, saying it was what his first wife had used to wash laundry. Unfortunately, his current wife was right next to him and didn't take too kindly to his recall of that memory.

She was rolling up our brochure as he was talking. The angrier she got—I could see her nostrils flaring from way in front of the group—the tighter and tighter she twisted the pamphlet. All I know is his daydream had him relaxed and smiling until the paper whapped him across the head."

With this, Toby gave a hearty laugh and Jenna chuckled. She had seen scenarios similar to this before on her watch at the museum. "I wish we were still working together, I would have liked to have seen it. You know, it might be fun to keep a record of times things like this happen."

Will reached across the lunch table and squeezed her hand. "I miss you there, too. I'm sure I don't leave the same impression you do. Most folks are happy with my tours, Mr. Levy has said so, but they lack your enthusiasm."

"Maybe you need more lessons," Jenna teased, her eyes alight with mischief.

Toby made a gagging sound next to her. "Please, I'm trying to choke down the food. Don't make it worse." He was only kidding and both Jenna and Will knew it. The limp burger he waved at them was his second.

"This isn't PDA, Toby. If you think the band room will be better, you can go see what Tina and Rob are up to, but I'll warn you—you'll need a strong stomach."

"Ugh, no thanks."

"I still think it's easier facing the groups with you there," Will said seriously. The word "face" caused Jenna to think about her visit.

"The more you do, the easier it will be. Um, you haven't seen anything weird at your place though, right?"

A frown pulled Will's brows down. "No. And my mom hasn't mentioned anything along those lines either. Jenna, I'm telling you, she's got a mad sense of intuition and she'd know if something was lurking in our house."

"You're right, you're right. I know. But the whole thing hasn't left me alone and it's been over a week since I went over. I still think about that face, especially since my family weekend amounted to nothing more than hanging around the house. I had too much time in my head."

"New dreams?" Toby asked with interest, pushing his empty tray towards the middle of the table.

"No, not really. Well, I keep dreaming about the country. Not like around here, like *Little House on the Prairie* kind of country. There's a general store and dirt roads. There's someone I'm angry about, but I can't remember more details. I wonder if it's me mentioning it now or thinking about it during the day that sets me up to dream about it later, or vice versa. I'm not sure what's coming first."

"But no man like you saw?"

"No. And I feel like we're getting the raw end of the deal seeing as how "our" weekend coming up is pretty much family weekend all over again, except with the grandparents." Jenna didn't mean to pout, it just frustrated her knowing her "Will weekend" was superseded by the way the holiday fell on the calendar. She wouldn't get the time with him she felt she deserved. His family had a rotating holiday schedule and it should have been in Pennellville for his Aunt Lee's turn. Instead, they had a whole family vacation planned out of town. Sometimes life was unfair.

"I know, but it is Thanksgiving. Mom and my aunts put the deposit on that hotel in Saratoga long before I knew you. Does it help to know we're in the same state? We'll really only be a few hours away."

The three of them had been talking about Will's road trip and there was a lot of explaining about what natural springs were. Will snuck a kiss on her knuckles to take the sting out of the situation.

"A little. It's just that I miss you already. It seems like forever until we'll have time for us. Of course I want you to enjoy your vacation. Your mom is so excited. The mineral baths sound like fun."

"Really, Jenna? It sounds like sitting in a small pool of warm cola to me," Toby said, leaning into the back of his chair. He apparently wasn't one for holistic relaxation methods. His arms were crossed around his thick chest as he digested his food. He tried not to be distracted by two boys arm wrestling at the table next to them. It seemed the lunch aides were letting things slide today. "You'd think the fizz would be flat by now."

"More like lemon-lime than cola if you're going to make that comparison," Will retorted. He refrained from saying anything when Brett Pulcher did an obnoxious victory dance when he won the match. Jenna actually rolled her eyes when Brett's girlfriend, Misty, swooned. "It's from a natural spring. People have been coming from all over the US to sit in that "soda" for years and years."

Toby sat up, leaning toward Will to be heard over the racket to their left.

"Jacobs, you wanna be next? Come on, I can take you."

Toby's attention shifted, his face scrunching up as if to show how ridiculous the idea was. "In your dreams. You might have taken on Pantalone there, but you couldn't win off your own mother."

The guys at table burst out laughing, and Brett's face took on some color. He gave Toby an unsolicited hand gesture before defending himself to his friends.

"That's not very nice," Jenna complained.

Toby shook his head. "I'm just busting on him, Jenna. He and I are the top wrestlers of Orchard Creek's team, and we're good buddies." He turned back to Will. "Dude, it's a spa. What guy goes for massages and facials?"

"The one who is always surrounded by only women relatives," Will replied dryly. "Don't knock it until you've tried it. I think we could convert you." Toby snorted while Will thought a moment. "Okay. You could do yoga instead?"

Toby's eyes reflected his amusement. "You're making my point for me."

Jenna pursed her lips while Will hid a smile. He was learning being friends with Toby was like having a brother. As annoying as he could sometimes get, Will enjoyed the camaraderie.

"Hush, Toby. Will's told me they have an auto museum."

"Now you're talking!"

Jenna started to make a comment as the bell rang. The group next to them hollered their goodbyes to each other, pumped up even more from not being reprimanded. Toby shook his head at the immaturity and grabbed his books. He balanced the plastic plate between two fingers as he started for the tray return. "Only two more classes. I can smell the sweet freedom of five alarm-free days already."

"Yeah, so can they," Jenna said, inclining her head. "What's on the agenda, Tobe?"

"Sleep in. Eat a lot of turkey, stuffing, and pie. Go to the gym. Definitely leftovers. Take a few naps. Why? What else is there to do?"

Toby looked so sincere Jenna sighed. She wondered when someone would catch his eye so he would get on par with the rest of his age group. "Apparently, nothing. See you when I see you."

"Have a good break, you two."

Jenna's demeanor deflated once again as soon as Toby left the table. Will made a decision that had been bouncing in his head. He didn't need to use his empathic ability to feel Jenna's mood, it was apparent to anyone who came near her. He rarely used his abilities to influence others, but her ruminating on this mystery man had her on edge. He couldn't stand seeing her in pain, so he concentrated on wooded trails and the smell of pine, like the nature trails they had gone to a few months back. He pushed the serenity from that experience outward towards her. The worry cleared and her face relaxed as she adjusted her purse on her shoulder.

"Maybe I'm overreacting with what the man means."

Will turned to her while the masses streamed around them to the hallways. "Maybe. I'll call later before we leave. Try to have a good holiday."

He leaned in. With Will so close, Jenna smiled and took in the citrus and sandalwood she knew she would miss. He glanced around for the room monitors before sneaking another quick kiss, this time on her cheek.

Five

THE HOLIDAY FINALLY passed. All the built-up hype of Thanksgiving seemed to hit the peak with Santa ending the Macy's Thanksgiving Day Parade—even if the meal wasn't done yet. The novelty of the holiday was gone by the time dessert was eaten and everyone had crashed in the living room to watch the football game. Jenna was glad her grandmother had finally left to go back home. She learned having Charlotte Cates stay a few days was completely different from a day visit.

It had been noisy in the Stevens house, and too much thick perfume lingered in the bathroom. It clashed with the BO that sometimes leaked out of her brother's room. Both she and Peter were run ragged being the hosts and entertainers, mostly fetching things the older people didn't want to get up and get themselves, and her normal routines were disrupted.

Family obligations, having parties, and visiting aunts, uncles, and friends almost every night, had worn her out.

Jenna felt she hadn't had a chance to rest. The holiday sure seemed longer when she was younger. It was hard for her to think about all the strange things she had seen right before break. She felt cut off. Will had called a few times each day but it wasn't the same.

It was a long week. In addition to all the work the teachers loaded on before break, the man's face returned. Jenna had almost convinced herself it was a one-time, fluky thing, but it happened again and again. The next time she had seen it was when she went to return a library book in town. Putting her book in the return slot, she glanced over at the new releases, thinking a few days off from school would be a good time to get in a good read. One book caught her attention, and she did a double take. The picture on the front of the hardcopy book was the side view of the man's face she had seen in Will's attic. When she looked again, it was gone. It was a history book about Abraham Lincoln and the recent debate over a possible disease he had had. It wasn't the man at all, not even close. This she forced to dismiss as a coincidence just because it was *a* man's face, and she had been sensitive about them lately. It got harder after that.

The time after that was while she was doing homework. Running her hands through her hair, a few loose strands fell on her notebook. A long blond, wavy hair landed on the white paper in almost the silhouette of the face. The letter "a" with an accent mark over it that she had written for French fit perfectly where the eye and eyebrow would look in a scowl. She was caught off guard. It always seemed to sneak up on her when her mind was elsewhere, causing her anxiety to increase exponentially.

The next evening at the museum was the worst. She was there, alone, unpacking some new antiques that just came in. After she took the empty boxes down to the basement, she went back to the desk. Writing down the year and places of origin of the delicate purses, she took a moment to sit back and stretch. Her back ached, and she looked around her trying to relax the muscles.

In the chrome fixture of the wall light, she saw him again. This time it wasn't a silhouette or a fuzzy outline, it was his face as if he was standing next to her. The distorted reflection was scary. His lips were pulled back to show yellowed, crooked teeth, and his green eyes were squinted to accusing slits. His thick, brown hair was in disarray, and his prominent chin looked prickly with stubble. The image of seeing her own face screaming next to his was more disturbing, and she jumped up to protect herself, nearly falling out of the chair. Whipping her head around, she found herself alone. No one was in the room with her. Tentatively, she looked up to the light fixture again. The warped reflection was only of her and the desk.

"I GOT THE phone!" Jenna yelled, rolling across her bed to grab the call. She had been sitting on her blankets with a book and got tied up in her bathrobe.

"Hi Jenna, it's Will." Just the timbre of his voice was enough to make her heart speed up.

"Can I be relieved to know you are in town?"

"Just came in the door and wanted to let you know. I didn't wake anyone, did I?"

"No, but it's close enough to our cut off at ten for calls. My parents are just starting to turn off the television and lights, complaining about being the only ones who are contributing to society, or something like that."

Will chuckled. "I've missed you so much. Did you manage to have fun for the holiday?"

"Sure. In the spirit of your encouragement, Pete and I invented a game to see which of us could tell what room grandma was in last. We tied, but Pete won the ice-breaker. He was able to list off the number of words she used that are completely out of vogue."

Will sighed on the other line. "How many?"

"Six. I forgot about "shindig." If we had double tied, it would have been sudden death with the number of times Uncle Howie tripped over her walker."

"I'm glad you persevered in my absence. Are you ready for tomorrow night? I made copies of our ceremony before we left."

"You did? Copies?"

"We all have binders with tabs separating the different ceremonies. This way you have your own papers to follow along."

"What's on the papers?" Jenna asked, lying back on the pillow to make herself more comfortable.

"Well, our books list what is needed for each specific ceremony because they vary."

"Like what?"

"Pomegranates, hardboiled eggs, myrrh oil, basil leaves, a piece of bread, chalice of water with flower petals, milk, and apples, to name a few. We have standard readings like the Opening Ritual Chant for opening the circle, and the Element Invocation which welcomes the elements from each quarter. We've long memorized those words, but you'd need them. We also have offering wishes and alter devotion pages. Each ceremony changes after that so we break down the papers specific to the ceremony. Otherwise, your binder would be too large to manage, things like that. We each have two Books of Shadows: the master and one for the working ceremony."

"It sounds like a lot."

"Don't get overwhelmed, you'll be fine. We do a meditation after we've opened the circle to help us relax and open our minds. My Aunt Diane writes beautiful poetry and she's written almost all the meditations. It's actually really refreshing. Then we go through the spells or rites or what have you. The paper lists what to say out loud and what to do in between. And we'll all help if you get lost." There was a pause. "That is, if you still want to do this. I don't ever want to pressure you into something—."

"No, Will, I'm okay. It doesn't sound too different from the psalm books we've read out of at church when we've gone. I'm still looking forward to it."

There was almost a sigh of relief on the other end, and it made Jenna's heart squeeze with affection.

"You know, my mom took comparative religion while in college—she had a double major—so she could probably translate what each reading equates to."

"I don't doubt it. I was just a little surprised to hear there is so much to a ceremony."

"There's purpose just like anything, I suppose. Oh, she's calling me to bring in my suitcase and the cooler so I have to go. I've missed you so much, Jenna. I needed you to know that."

"I've missed you too. Welcome home." For whatever reason, Jenna slept especially well that night.

WITH HOMEWORK DONE and new fiction book read, the minutes she had counted down reached zero. She was glad it was finally Friday and she could see Will. It was also his family's Full Moon Ceremony. Maybe she could muster some courage while she was at it, and talk to Will about the repeating image. She was stumped even with the oddities that had always run about in her head; first in her dreams and then at the museum. Those seemed normal for her as they had happened for so long.

This man was something completely different. Obviously, Jenna didn't share a resemblance. And this felt darker. Much darker. Jenna wasn't sure what the face meant, but she knew its intention wasn't benign like finding a handkerchief or special candle. The only connection she could come up with were the pictures Will and his mom found in their basement that referred to October first. They had trouble then, that's for sure, but nothing since. That was also when Jonas was sent back to the other realm. This man looked nothing like him.

Sulis had once said Jenna was just more open to passing and intersecting entities. Other than the museum, though, that's all they ever were, just passing. Were the gifts Sulis said she had somehow growing? Were her past experiences allowing her to become more susceptible to everything else that passed through a thin spot of a veil? First her dreams, then the museum, and now everywhere? She was becoming scared to admit to herself she was vulnerable. Maybe it was because she felt there was no safe place anymore.

Jenna knew Will was used to the unusual, but when it happened to the same person over and over, she was unsure what he'd think of her. She never wanted to be high maintenance. Maybe he would think enough is enough and that she was too odd.

Friday evening finally arrived without any more faces popping up. As much as Jenna was looking forward to the night, her stomach squirmed in nervousness at ruining the evening by mentioning her newest problem. She knew it would be a busy time, so she scrapped the idea of bringing it up. She decided to let the evening just happen, and if there was a quiet opportunity to discuss it with Will, she would tell him.

Will greeted her at the sound of the doorbell, and she stepped inside somewhat apprehensively. The stereo was on again, the bell-like soprano voice clear from the speaker by the entryway. There were cars outside, but she didn't hear any voices. Before she could wonder if his aunts were inside, she remembered how soundproofed the rooms were. Will hugged

Jenna and kissed her quickly on the cheek. She hesitated after taking her shoes off.

"They already know you're here and are dying to meet you, so come in."

Jenna walked into the green room and saw a flash of silver hair from the kitchen.

Will beamed as he held her hand. "They are very excited, and they seem to be a little impatient. Are you sure you really want to subject yourself to this?" His face was already flushed. As much as the playful smile teased her, there was a tightness in his eyes.

"Yes," Jenna smiled back, a little intimidated. They walked through the green and red rooms into the kitchen entryway, the music following them from the speakers set around the house, where all eyes focused on her. Sulis immediately saw the tension Jenna was holding and came around the island. Her long black velvet dress swayed back and forth as she warmly put her arm around Jenna's shoulders.

"Don't worry, I told them to tone it down a little," she mock-whispered by her ear.

"For the first time, anyway," corrected the woman stepping around the island. "Welcome to ceremony, Jenna. I'm Mina, Sulis's second oldest sister." Mina smiled as she hugged Jenna, the long, deep red, lacy, butterfly sleeves of her dress wrapping around and obscuring her arm. Mina had gray eyes like the sky after a storm that crinkled up in a friendly way when she smiled. Her long, dangling, silver earrings shined in the light. She was the only one who had allowed the natural progression of time to take hold and boasted thick, straight, silver hair. It framed her face and was bobbed to just below her ears. Mina led her into the kitchen as if they were the best of friends. Jenna stood at the table full of food and tentatively took a carrot stick from the decorative platter, scooping up some dip. It was French onion, her favorite. Sulis went back to the counter to get her a glass for a drink, and another woman took the glass from her and went to the freezer for ice.

The woman sitting at the table with a small note card and pen looked at Jenna. "I'm Diane, the first of the mold. So, we've been trying to figure out what has the most potential to blend in a dish undetected, eye of newt or slime of worm. Which do you think?"

Jenna stood there, speechless, no longer chewing, with a shocked expression on her face. The ladies waited for an answer, expectant and serious. They wouldn't really use slime of worm, would they? *Would* they? She knew they were witches. Now she was scared.

"That's not funny, Aunt D. Stop," Will scolded, pulling Jenna behind him protectively as he spoke to his aunt. The rest of the ladies sniggered to themselves, clearly in on the joke, and obviously, not repentant. "Jenna, they can't be good for very long. I'm apologizing for them already."

Diane smirked a devilish grin which melted into a genuine smile. "I'm sorry, I couldn't resist. Ooh, but that was fun! Consider yourself initiated. Sorry. Truly, it's a pleasure to finally meet you. We've all heard so much about you." Diane set down the pen she was using to write out a recipe and reached around the table to shake her hand. Every finger had a different ring on it. All were silver, some had red stones, and some had green.

The designs ranged from a pentacle to an Irish Claddagh friendship ring.

"Thanks, Diane. I guess that makes me the one who broke the mold," Sulis interjected sarcastically, bringing over a tray with cheeses and pepperoni.

Will ignored the remark. "Aunt Diane is only the oldest by a year. She's our doctor." Jenna's eyes widened in surprise, and Will continued. "She has her doctorate in sociology, anyway. I think she likes to use that to pump herself up sometimes with us little people. Actually, it is impressive that she put herself back through school and got her degree later in life."

"Later in life, hah, he's too kind," Diane demurred. "I was fifty-four. But it's never too late for something new," she shrugged. When she smiled her facial features most resembled Mina's. Diane's hair was baby-fine, dark brown with reddish-brown undertones, and layered short with thin bangs that curled on their own. Her almond-shaped eyes were a faded hazel, and her nose was strong, but petite. Even though she was sitting, Jenna could see she wore a black dress similar to Sulis's.

A younger-looking woman in a long, clinging, dark gray dress handed the glass with ice in it to Jenna. "Hi, Jenna, I'm Whitty, nice to meet you." Whitty was thinner than the rest and had blond hair to the middle of her neck that was neatly styled and in fashion. Her eyes were a bright bluish-gray with long lashes, and her nose was long and straight, unlike her sisters. She wore two simple silver chains, one that rested on her neck above the scoop neckline of her dress, and one that delicately hung down lower. They accented her gown perfectly.

Jenna shook hands and started to relax. It was impossible

not to feel welcome; the genuine friendliness exuded from everyone.

The last of the women, wearing a rich, solid green blouse and skirt, set down a bowl of dip and walked to Jenna from the other end of the table. For a moment Jenna thought she had already been sitting down. "I'm Lee, the normal one," the shortest of the group said with an easy smile. Her green outfit brought out the green in her hazel eyes and made them pop. She, too, had short hair, hers more auburn than brown. It held a wave that fit against her head and forehead and reminded Jenna of a flapper's hairstyle.

It seemed none of the ladies hit quite five feet in height. Lee was rebuked by several sisters but shushed them off with an infectious laugh. She asked Jenna questions about the museum, truly interested.

Will pulled up an extra chair by Jenna while they all snacked. It was loud, just as he had promised. All his aunts were a real hoot, uncouth and uninhibited. The conversations overlapped and blended, never lagging. Will was right about having good reason to be scared, but she was agreeing it was more so for him. They had almost two decades of dirt on Will they could dish at any time, and they did. There were no reservations.

Jenna was included and contributed when she was able to stop laughing long enough. The topics jumped from what Jenna had experienced at the museum to why men were the only ones who could go shirtless in public when they weren't the gender who had hot flashes. Jenna learned a lot more than she probably felt comfortable with, but the women never made her feel out of place, even when each showed off their latest tattoos. Jenna laughed, thinking how completely opposite

Will's family was from hers. First, because she couldn't image her mother and aunts getting tattoos, and second, there was no way they'd be sitting around so casually talking about these topics with such a lack of embarrassment.

Jenna was even invited to their women-only hot-tub club at his Aunt Lee's house which she admitted she wasn't ready for. Jenna preferred wearing a bathing suit.

"Can you feel the difference in energy around Jenna?" Sulis asked her sisters when there was a lull in the conversations. Sulis was casually leaning against the sink, a glass of soda in her hand. Jenna frowned and looked over at Will, expecting him to now reprimand his mother. Instead, he nodded as he looked at his aunts.

"Yes, I can," Mina agreed. The others concurred.

The frown on Jenna's face deepened. "What do you mean?"

"Everything in the world emits energy. If you study to be aware of that which is around you, you can distinguish the differences," Diane explained as she brushed crumbs from the table into her hand and got up to go to the trash.

Whitty adjusted her necklace chain so the clasp was behind her neck. "Your spiritual energy is very strong. Perhaps that's why you channel so easily," she surmised.

"It's also a good reason to learn more about your gifts, so that you are grounded to protect yourself," Mina suggested. Heads nodded all around.

"Protect myself?" Jenna was confused.

Diane looked at Jenna, her hands animated to make her point. "You have channeled at the museum. Like a light switch and a bulb with a wire between the two, you are the conductor.

Since everything has energy, it is important to allow the energy to pass through you without taking your own energy with it. Have you had any formal training?"

Jenna looked over to Will who shook his head. "No, I don't know very much about what I can do. It just happens."

"Raw talent like that is truly a gift! I'm anxious to see what happens when she's concentrating on it," Lee said, petting Rommy who was weaving around her ankles.

Seamlessly, the food and drinks were picked up and put away, and the conversations changed to the reason they were there. The mood settled into a more reverent tone. Ceremony was about to start.

Six

*J*ENNA WATCHED AS Will and his family began collecting the items they needed: salt, a piece of bread, and glass of milk along with their personal notebooks they called their Book of Shadows. Each was decorated to her own personal taste with pictures, poems and drawings. They needed just a few more things before heading upstairs to the ceremony room. Will admitted he left the copies he made for Jenna on his dresser, and wanting to feel useful, as well as read them over beforehand, Jenna had offered to get them.

Jenna went up the main door staircase and hurried down the hall, trying to remember which door was Will's, and proud of herself for being able to find her way. She was anxious not to hold them up and kept repeating in her head what she was to get from his room. She knew she had the right door when she turned on the light and the blue curtains faced back at her. Her head turned to the mirror as she caught her own movement in her peripheral vision. She immediately fumbled backwards.

There, along with the reflection of Will's neatly made bed, was a watery image of a man a decade or so older than her father. Jenna gasped, turning her head quickly to her left to him straight on, and let out a startled scream. His face was the same one that had been stalking her since her first visit here. Then, just like looking at a water mirage in the road, he faded into nothingness.

A transient thought popped into her head. She had once heard that a person having a heart attack had a feeling of impending doom. She felt that way now. She wasn't having a heart attack, yet, but her heart was pounding away in her chest, attempting to achieve one condensed beat. She stepped into the room, grabbing the plastic binder off Will's dresser. As she turned back toward the mirror she froze as the image returned. She spun again, drawing the papers to her chest as if they were a shield. This time the man smiled, but it wasn't a happy smile. It was an evil, satisfied sneer that spread across his face. He was standing still but seemed tense, ready to strike. Jenna let out an ear-piercing scream as she charged for the door, slamming it loudly behind her. A man's laugh echoed from inside the room.

Jenna had just gotten to the end of the hallway when Will caught up to her on his way up, startling her.

"Good Goddess, Jenna, look at you. What's wrong?"

"It's, it was, the man. I saw the man, like a holographic image, just standing there. Then he was gone," she managed to say around her shallow breathing. When she pointed towards his room her whole hand trembled.

"What's going on?" Sulis asked as she and the other ladies reached the landing from the stairs. Lee and Mina were the last to come up and had been discussing the pros and cons of a roasted turkey versus one marinated in a brine solution. The mood sobered as Will gathered Jenna in a one-armed hug. His binder was held in his other hand.

"Now can we tell her?" an exasperated Will asked. With her head down, Jenna nodded. "Jenna saw a man up here just now. Remember when she came over for dinner and we fell through the thin wall up in the attic? It knocked the wind out of her and she saw a face there while she was trying to catch her breath. She said she just saw it again before it disappeared."

"In my house?" Sulis asked, a note of protectiveness in her voice.

"Yes, in Will's room." Without a word, the women started walking towards the room with purpose. Jenna, feeling more in control, followed behind them, telling them the details as they asked.

They all stood in the open doorway of Will's room, except Will and Jenna, who were in the hallway between both bedrooms. Ideas and thoughts were volleyed back and forth, as everyone stared into the empty room.

"I just can't imagine why Jenna would have seen something like that here."

"Sissy, maybe she's picking up a stray entity from the past," Diane guessed.

"Then why did it look so irate?" Whitty replied. No one had a good answer.

Jenna's cheeks were slowly warming from pale white to

pink from the encounter. She still felt jittery. Will held her tightly, trying to get the shaking to subside. She wasn't used to feeling this way other than at the museum.

"I just don't understand. Something this sinister is in my home, and I have been completely unaware of it," Sulis sighed.

"You've always had a knack for that. I've never had a good feel for spaces myself," admitted Diane studying the corners by the window.

"Not everyone can read several books a day like you, Diane," Lee retorted. "Is it his room itself?"

"No, Jenna saw his face up in the attic," Will interjected, breaking away from Jenna.

"That was just the first time," Jenna said quietly. "I've seen his image all over the place since then."

There was a moment of surprised silence. "Why didn't you tell me about them?" Will asked, puzzled.

Jenna couldn't meet his eyes. "You kinda looked at me like I was off my rocker when I told you in the attic."

"I would always take you seriously about things like this. I thought you would know that." Jenna could tell Will was offended and hurt, but at the moment didn't know how to fix the situation.

"All's quiet now," Sulis said, turning the light off and closing the door.

"Well, if Jenna saw him upstairs first, let's make our way to the attic. You mentioned you had broken out part of a wall?" asked Mina. She was the most motherly of the sisters and rubbed Jenna's back soothingly as she walked back into the hallway.

"It's nothing special, just four bare walls, some blankets and a basin," Will clarified.

Once there, they went up with Will one at a time so as not to put too much stress on the delicate flooring and looked around at the makeshift bedroom. "You know, this area of New York was very popular with the Underground Railroad," Whitty suggested as she stepped down off the last stair.

"That has a lot of potential," Lee agreed.

"This could have been a safe house that assisted escaped slaves on their way from slave-owned states to freedom in Canada. Maybe—but no—the man you saw wasn't African American, was he Jenna?" asked Diane.

"No."

"Hmm, well, maybe the owner of the house was a conductor, someone who physically moved the slaves from safe house to safe house, helping, and got caught and hasn't found peace," Diane suggested.

"This house is very old. There are a lot of possibilities," Lee added.

"And none we will probably know for sure right now. It'll have to wait for another day. Time is wasting," Sulis stated as she looked once more at the doorway to the attic, then turned, resigned, to go back downstairs. "Will, are you coming? We want to start ceremony sometime tonight," she yelled behind her.

Jenna had been standing quietly off to the side while everyone had taken a look. She had finally calmed down and now just felt tired. "I'll go up and see what's taking him so long," she offered, climbing the stairs slowly.

"That would be helpful. I'm going back down to make sure we'll all set. Ceremony, in five minutes, Will! Get a move on."

"What are you doing up here?" Jenna asked as she cleared the threshold. She squinted to see Will who was half visible by the broken-out wall. His back was to her. "Will, what is it?" She became concerned when he didn't answer her right away. For just a moment, Jenna became scared and hugged her arms around her body.

"There's something else," Will whispered. He had not turned around.

Jenna's restlessness increased. She walked towards him, stumbling in the uneven path. When she reached Will, he turned to her, back inside the blanket of light thrown by the bare bulb. Again, like a few weeks before, the familiar smirk of mischief played at the corners of his mouth. His eyes were almost black, dilated from the darkened room or excitement, or both, she was unsure. Searching his face, Jenna was confused. It wasn't until she looked down at his hands that she understood his expression. He had found something up there. It was a long-handled knife. He pushed past her to take a closer look under the light.

"Check this out! It was stuck into the wall, on an angle like a coat hook," Will began but broke off with an intake of breath. Jenna did the same when the light shown on the knife's details. At first look it was long, about sixteen inches and obviously made of wood with variances of both light and dark brown. A gnarled knot was at the end of the handle that reminded Jenna vaguely of a joint at the end of a bone. The straight blade looked scratched in the glare of the light on the metal. Upon closer inspection, it was anything but an ordinary knife.

"Will and Jenna, we are not waiting for you! You cannot cross the circle once we've started, and I will not allow a door to be cut!" Sulis's strong voice reached them faintly from the beginning of the hallway below. Like children caught being naughty, they both jumped, the knife disappearing behind Will's back with a whooshing sound as it cut through the air. He looked up at Jenna, her face creased with worry.

"We'll come back for it later," Will promised. Jenna shook her head, realizing he misunderstood her concern.

"But your mom should know—" she began.

"It's safe here. My mom's too heavy to come up here at all."

"Will, after the stuff that happened at the museum with the Ouija board, I'd feel more comfortable if—"

"All is right, Jenna," he said, cutting her off. "No worries!" He set the knife down and put an old blanket over it. Grabbing her hand, he pulled her from the room quickly before she could reply. It was so unlike him, Jenna wasn't sure if he was frustrated with her over the situation, or worried about being late for ceremony.

Leading her by the hand, Will and Jenna stepped into the darkened ceremony room. Even after he had given her a rundown of what this ceremony entailed, she had lost the time to acquaint herself with her copies. At first, she couldn't properly concentrate, preoccupied with the knife and how Will's demeanor changed when he found it. She didn't have time to deconstruct all that concerned her.

A few candles on the altar were already lit. Jenna took in her surroundings and her curiosity helped to keep her other thoughts at bay. She was happy to realize she knew what most of the items on the altar were for. The candles and pentacle, the small boat of salt, and athames were now familiar to her. In addition to the small ceramic figurines of the panther and owl that Jenna remembered seeing during her first tour of the house, they were now joined by a bumblebee, a faux fur covered polar bear, a clay gazelle, and a small wooden goat.

"Those are our spirit animals. Mine is the goat, Diane's is the polar bear, and Whitty's is the gazelle," Mina explained as she watched Jenna.

"Don't forget my bumblebee," Lee added as she settled into her chair.

"And those? Let me guess, Will's is the panther, and Sulis has the owl," Jenna deduced.

Will smiled as he cupped his hand to brush away the hair from his face. "How'd you know my spirit guide is a panther?"

"It seemed to fit when I thought about it. Plus, Sulis is just about the smartest person I know," Jenna said, shrugging. Cackles all around the table responded to her opinion.

It took a moment for the women to find the same page in each of their books. Sitting particularly close to Will, Jenna was able to hold his hand which made her feel a little better, while she balanced the small, three-ringed binder on her lap. Then, incense and more candles were lit, they spurged with the salt, and then stood to open the circle and call the elements.

"East is air. Its many fragrances fill our lungs to sing and laugh and encourage. Please join us, air!"

They turned from the yellow candle of east to the south. Will and the women raised their athames as Sulis continued, lighting the red quarter candle. "Fire. The flames that burn in the hearts of every being, giving us drive, passion and warmth, welcome fire!"

They moved clockwise, or deosil as Will called it, so Sulis could ask for water to join them. Jenna raised her hand with everyone else and thought about the cleansing and refreshing abilities water had.

"Earth that is our home, where our feet find the foundation to seek out happiness and family, please join us, earth!" The women turned to the altar in the middle as Will winked at her to do the same. Maybe it was the sacredness of their circle, but Will had finally calmed down and was acting more and more like himself. Jenna was glad.

They raised their athames once again as Sulis spoke the words to summon spirit. Then they all sat in their chairs, flipping through their binders, their Book of Shadows, to the guided imagery. Everyone but Diane closed their eyes.

Jenna breathed deeply to let her body and thoughts ease. She followed the meditation and listened to the soothing monotone words that formed the image of a cool forest in her head. It was difficult to let herself relax at first, but she was eventually able to when she let that small part of worry go. Deep breaths in and controlled exhaling slowed her heart rate and calmed her breathing. The tension in the muscles of her arms and legs were pulled away leaving her feeling light and free. Doing what the meditation asked, she directed the stress to flow from her fingers and feet, grounding herself. She felt weightless yet at the same time, anchored to those surrounding her.

When they were invited to reopen their eyes, Jenna felt at

peace, her eyes taking in her surroundings. The bland room seemed to blend into nothingness as the candles made a cozy area all its own. The creamy, ivory glow and the smell of patchouli were familiar. She glanced to Will whose attention, for once, was not on her.

From the very first instant, she had felt a kind of attraction to him. Even when she was upset, he could calm her right down, and she knew it had nothing to do with his empathic abilities. She always thought a part of it was her crush on him. Now, within this circle with her attention focused, she could discern it wasn't just Will, part of it was his energy. Was this what his aunts were talking about? Sitting here quietly, she realized she could feel the power that each woman emitted. It ricocheted back to her from the center of the altar. Jenna could only compare it to static cling but without the physical joining of fabrics. It was like an electromagnetic charge with an impulse to be drawn to them.

Everyone was absorbed in turning to the next section. Jenna noted the resemblance of the women, mostly diminutive and heavy set, with eye color that ranged from blue-gray to hazel. Even their smiles were a little crooked. Each was slightly different but part of the same puzzle with Sulis sharing the most in common in facial features with Whitty. It was obvious they all were sisters; their personalities were cut from the same distinctive cloth. Jenna could also imagine Sylvia at her altar using the stubs of ancient candles to do the same, well over a hundred years ago. The way the candles showed use had Jenna wondering about the types of ceremonies. Something just dawned on her and she frowned.

"May I ask a question?"

"Of course. Always," Sulis answered.

"I probably should have asked beforehand what a Full Moon ceremony is about."

Everyone looked to Whitty who shrugged her shoulders. "I am the moon witch, I guess. I associate with the element of water."

"And... you lost me," Jenna admitted.

"The moon moves the tides, my dear. The phases of the moon are important to Pagans. Most phases last about three days. When the moon grows and increases in size it's a safe time to practice, especially for spells that involve fresh starts. Ceremonies for a full moon are called Esbats and are a particularly good time for magic."

"I see," Jenna said. "So, working with the moon is helpful to what you try to achieve."

Sounds of dissent were heard in the circle. "No, not all the time," Lee answered.

"When the moon is not watching over us, a dark moon, it's best not to work magic. Too much potential for our intentions to go wrong," Whitty clarified. Her sisters all nodded.

"Actually, spells are extremely potent then, especially those that are destructive or release," Sulis added. "Personally, we don't recommend doing witchcraft at all then because energies could get muddled."

"Full moons rituals are almost as powerful because the moon has reached its highest peak in the phase," Mina said, handing Jenna a new taper candle and lighting it.

Jenna continued to follow along, noting the hardest part was finding specific pages since everyone bounced around instead of reading in order. It was also a bit unnerving to be sure the binder didn't slide off her legs while not setting anything on fire.

The small area grew warmer. Pulses of energy flowed around and through her. It made her think of Walt Disney's idea of sprites. The residual vigor left an afterglow of vague designs on the inside of her eyes when she closed them. It felt like an intense, almost heat-like nudge of pressure on her from all four directions that sometimes resonated through her. It doubled next to her as it linked and bound her to Will who was at her side.

A loud hiss—a brief sizzling sound next to her ear—startled Jenna back into the here and now, and her eyes opened. The notebook fell to the floor at the same time a panicked look crossed each of the faces around her.

Seven

"WHAT…?" BEGAN JENNA, looking at the others. She was thinking there must be some part in the ritual where the candles are blown out as someone had just done with hers. It was only when she noticed that Mina was too far away that she started to feel uneasy. She was sure someone had just been at her shoulder; she had felt the invisible wave of coolness push against her as if someone had walked by her quickly and very closely. The puff of air by her ear was tangible because it had moved her hair.

Squeezing Will's hand with her right, Jenna looked at the candle in her left, the curls of smoke rising slowly, drawn to the center of the altar. The white wisps dissipated into thicker fibers and circled around with purpose. Jenna's attention went to Will as he squeezed her hand too tightly.

"Does anyone else see this?" he asked no one in particular.

"Yes, we do," Mina answered. All eyes were on the shape of a face forming in the smoke from Jenna's extinguished candle.

"That's him! That's the man's face I see," Jenna whispered, horrified. No one had moved, yet the threads spun and wound on, animating the expression on the face into a sneer that seemed to be looking directly at Jenna. It then dissipated into the air as a thin sheet before disappearing completely.

The room was quiet while each woman tried to figure out what had happened. Will's brow furrowed with concern. They closed the circle shortly after that.

There was a moment or two when no one spoke. The second passed, and everyone rose. Even though Jenna had never attended a full ceremony before, she knew the silence was uncommon.

"I think I need to keep a pair of readers with me, it's getting harder to see the words," Lee admitted. She opened her large three-ringed binder to the red pencil bag that was there, and zipped her athame in the pouch. Jenna was sure she had the same bag in blue in her school backpack.

"It happens to the best of us, old timer," Mina soothed, patting her younger sister on the head. Lee squinted her eyes and made a face, clearly biting her tongue.

"Stop joking. I need...I need some answers," Will demanded, parsing his words as he put his Book of Shadows on one of the chairs. "That has never happened during our ceremonies. What was that? Why did it happen tonight?"

"I don't have any answers," Sulis replied, looking tired. Her sisters shook their heads to agree.

"I don't think everything can be explained right away," Diane began, as she put her hand on Will's shoulder.

"Aunt D, nothing is being explained! This space was cleansed. What comes to us after we've opened the circle should only be what we've invited. He wasn't invited. Does this mean we were exposed? Is Jenna safe, mom?"

"Yes, Will, Jenna is safe. We all are. We were all guarded in the circle. It is cast to protect us; our safe zone. Whatever that was, was on the outside."

Lee sighed, as she took the candle snuffer and began to put out the rest of the candles. "That doesn't particularly make me feel warm and fuzzy."

"Nor I," Sulis agreed, setting a plate on the altar. "Everyone take a cookie, we need to ground." She then picked up the plate and chalices, "but that doesn't mean we weren't safe."

"Has anything like that happened in any ceremony you've had?" Will asked, after taking a bite. The faces that looked back at him gave him his answer. His mother and half his aunts did a good job of studying their treat. Each had chosen a molasses cookie. Concern shown in Aunt Mina's eyes as she watched Jenna, and Aunt Diane just looked tired.

"No, not in all the years of our practice, but just because we can't explain it this second doesn't mean we won't find the answers. We'll make calls, consult others and do some research," Diane responded. She started to put some of the items away.

"We weren't going to just let her go home without giving her some information. We needed to close circle before we could even start," Whitty said, finding her water bottle by her feet.

"We just need time, Will."

"Jenna, are you okay?" Mina asked, rubbing Jenna's arm.

"I feel responsible," Jenna blurted out. She hadn't tasted the sugar cookie at all. She turned to Will. "Like when we summoned those bad spirits from the Ouija board at the museum at the end of September and they all crossed over on October first." Will and the ladies all began talking at once to pacify her, but Jenna brushed them off. "You haven't seen the man here, I have. It was something at *my* back and blew out *my* candle. It's me. Negativity follows me."

"No," Sulis ordered, her hands full of candles. "Don't allow yourself to think that way. You just happen to be a natural conduit to energy which doesn't discriminate. I've known that since I bumped into you at the Wal-Mart. It can be both good and bad. What you may need to do sooner rather than later is learn to shield and block so the negative energy can't linger around you so closely. We need to train you up so you can control it."

"Yes! And I know you'll be amazing," Will added.

Jenna had little confidence in what he was saying until she happened to glance up at Mina when Will was talking and caught a whisper of a smile on her face. Maybe she should trust them to help her. She hadn't felt safe, but his family was sincere in their offers. She just wanted so badly not to make things worse for everyone.

She needed to talk with Will. There were too many things she didn't understand. With no time to return to the attic or be alone, the night had ended with many more questions than answers.

JENNA SHIVERED UNDER her covers again, as she had each time she thought about the last few minutes of the ceremony. She suddenly felt very alone.

Across town, Will should have been in bed hours ago, but he couldn't sleep. It was great that Jenna had joined him in something so important to him. He just couldn't appreciate it right now. Other than during ceremony, his thoughts had gone haywire since being in the attic. The attic, the knife, the canning cellar, everything now held a mystery he needed to learn. Just like with Sylvia's athame and now this knife, he should have told his mother about them. He had no intention of that, not right now, anyway. She didn't need to know everything yet. He wanted to research this blade a bit online first so he had more info. He had screwed up with the Ouija board, indeed, and the apple through the window, but he was going to pay more attention now. He could barely think of anything else when Jenna was around, but he was concentrating very hard on separating the part of his brain that lived and breathed Jenna from the part that had to be rational. He wasn't going to be so preoccupied that he would goof up again.

He thought back to Halloween night when he and Jenna discovered Sylvia's athame. They had just finished putting Amelie's remains to rest. That was right after witnessing a spell that carried smoke from the turquoise candle through the orchard and into the museum. Everyone had then gone back inside and split up to be sure everything was quiet. He and Jenna went upstairs to the Loft area to be sure nothing was out of order. There on Sylvia's old altar was an athame that hadn't been prior to their ritual. Will already knew what Sylvia's ceremonial knife looked like. It was hers.

Once they discovered it, Will had promised Jenna he would put it away somewhere safe. That was the best compromise he could make. He didn't plan on keeping it a secret forever. But he also adamantly disagreed to tell anyone else who experienced Halloween at the museum that night. Jenna wanted him to, but it was just too intriguing. He thought he would look it over and try a few things. No, nothing beyond what he was taught or practiced. He honored and respected his mother too much to do otherwise. Lesson learned. However, no matter how close they were, he felt he needed some space to learn on his own. He was practically out of high school. Almost. And now, with the discovery of the new knife, something else discouraged him from showing anyone, and he agreed with it.

He knew he should have been a little apprehensive when he finally snuck the secret knife back into his room and took a good look at it in the bright light. At first glance, it appeared to be a dark wooden handle, but the light color variations were actually skulls and faces that had been carved and burnt into the wood. Some were tiny, about the size of a dime. The largest were thumb-sized. The details for faces so little on one piece of wood only six inches long were incredible. Not friendly faces either; these seemed to want to moan or scream. These skulls covered the length of the handle.

The knot at the end was called the rear bolster, Will remembered. He had studied antique weapons for years and was pleased to find he remembered quite a bit. The part that joins the blade to the handle, the bolster, was also somehow carved with dozens of skulls. Further up was the guard between the handle and blade. From the heavy weight of the knife and its particular color, Will assumed it was made out of silver. It had an intricate web with a large spider on the pommel or center of the guard. The guard was used as a counterweight on any reputable fencing sword or knife. In addition to protecting the hand of the fighter, it helped balance the weight of the handle with the weight of the blade so the fighter could use it well.

He held his finger underneath, and the knife balanced evenly. So, it wasn't a novelty piece; this was the real deal. He had already known that, but this made it official. It did make him nervous to see how the design on the silver pommel grew outward to the quillon, the ends of the guard. The pommel was the shape of a spider. The lower body of the spider itself was a round, whitish, opaque stone. He'd known right away it was a moonstone. The quillons were the silver legs of the spider. They curled around towards the blade as if to dare a competitor to come closer.

The blade itself was beveled, almost triangular in shape, etched in writings he didn't understand and symbols he had seen before but for the moment was too jazzed to remember where. It was scored with spiders and skulls on it as well. Its sides and end had small nicks throughout; this knife wasn't for show, it had seen action.

Will shuddered and put the knife down. He knew this did not belong with the Wicca he practiced. It didn't stand for anything on the right side of the Law, he snorted to himself in the quiet room. This was a knife of darkness. Still, it attracted him, and he picked it back up without thinking about it. It made him feel strong. Somewhere, in the back of his mind, something screamed at him to stop and get rid of it. He ignored it.

He got up from the bed, fluidly, without the cognizant thought to do so, and went towards his closet where Sylvia's athame was stashed in an old shoebox. He put both knives together. A white flash of light blinded him momentarily as they touched. The light was cold. He felt it enter his eyes, where it began to creep slowly into his brain before free-falling. It filled his whole body with an icy chill that dissipated just as quickly as it had come on. Will shuddered once, not particularly bothered by it. He put his summer shorts on top of the box and closed the closet door without making a sound. Now he had two treasures to play with, learn about, explore.

"Cops and robbers, cops and robbers," he muttered to himself as he absentmindedly rubbed his thumb against his first finger. He had almost everything he needed. All his thoughts were in order. Will was vaguely aware they seemed to be tilted on their side, somehow askew, fuzzy although he did not feel dizzy. It was something indiscernible about how his mind worked that was no longer the same. Anyway, no one needed to know about this at all, not even Jenna. Especially not her, he amended half a second later. In fact, she might be the one pebble in his boot. She seemed a force to be reckoned with, although she had no idea how to control her abilities.

Will climbed into bed and stared at the ceiling. This evening had made him very happy. A smile spread across his face, pulling up only on the left side of his mouth and eye. The right side remained a bit flat as if the voluntary movement didn't apply to it. There was so much to do, and as always, so little time. It was less than a month, but it was enough. It wasn't like he had never done this before.

In the next room, Sulis was tossing and turning. It was a hideous nightmare. With a ringing in her ears, she was running through the darkness, but she was not able to travel quickly enough. She moved through each dim room that had two doorways, running faster, but gaining less ground when she looked behind her. It was the way dreams worked, although this did not feel like a dream. The fear grew. Where was the pillar? Why couldn't she find the small delicate yellow crystal she needed to save herself?

It was also not a dream she could manipulate. Sulis had practiced lucid dream control for years to direct what she wanted to happen. It took a long time to have awareness of dreaming to do this. She could wake up from a particular dream for a drink of water or go to the bathroom and get right back into it. It was not so now. There was an element missing or an extra one present. Sulis couldn't stay on top of it long enough to demand control.

It was barely bright enough to see where she was going, but she knew she had to keep moving. She began to scream when enough light shown through for her to see who had been chasing her. The image changed and morphed, becoming Will. She froze where she stood, and he approached her with his arm raised with a silver glint and a sneer on his face. His arm came down and coldness penetrated her body at the same time a curtain of darkness covered her eyes, and she knew she was dead.

Sulis awoke and shuddered at the icy sweat that covered her whole body. The house remained quiet. "Good," she whispered to herself. She hated to think of having to explain to Will what had made her yell out. It was embarrassing. She hadn't had nightmares before, at least not since her husband's funeral, and especially none like this.

The dream remained very clear in her mind, but Sulis couldn't remember what Jenna had to do with any of it. Somewhere Jenna's image was now forefront in her mind, and she was repelled by it. But why? Had she been dreaming of Jenna, too? The violence and feeling of insecurity upset her, and she knew that had carried over from the evening's events. Jenna had only been in her home twice, on two separate instances. For a moment, she was frustrated with the young woman. Sulis loved this place. Something had been let loose in her home the moment Jenna had stepped foot here, she was sure of it. Whatever she carried about her apparently wasn't limited to just the building down the road. Or was it?

Sulis got up from the bed and made her way in the glow of the bright moonlight to her closet for a dry nightgown. After changing, she got back into bed, trying to warm herself from the chill. She was sure it had only been the museum and that Jenna was merely a pawn, but now she doubted her own ability and beliefs. She had always been able to *feel* things. Why couldn't she feel her own home? Was she wrong about Jenna, too?

She thought back to the first time she met Jenna. The girl plowed into her in the store, knocking all her items to the floor. It was when they both reached for the same thing that their hands touched, and Sulis was jolted by the energy the girl possessed. She had an untapped talent to channel but was absolutely unaware of it or what she was able to do with it. Jenna's innocence and this powder keg of talent were what peaked her attention. So, was there more to it that Sulis didn't know?

The end of the bed jiggled, and Sulis drew in a startled breath of air. Tiny feet walked over her legs up to her chin. His ears were back, irritated.

"Hello, Rommy," Sulis greeted him with a pat. She scooped him up and held him close, letting his soft fur warm her face and neck. She was puzzled. Rommy never came in her room at night. He always slept with Will.

Maybe she should put a stop to Jenna's visits here until she figured it out. But Will was so smitten with her. It warmed Sulis's heart to see how silly he got when he was around her or talked about her. It reminded Sulis of her first love, and her thoughts again turned to her husband. She settled back on the bed, trying to concentrate on the comforting memories that were all she had left. The remnants of the nightmare were still there, but Sulis had always been very good at willing her mind to do what she wanted. She would analyze the dream later. It didn't feel like a need for more control in her life, that didn't add up. She felt comfortable with who and where she was. It made no sense at all unless she had been wrong about Jenna from the moment she had first met her.

Eight

ENNA ACTUALLY LOOKED forward to school. She wasn't
able to see Will the whole weekend because it was her
family weekend, and she hadn't been able to talk to
him on the phone either. Will had stuttered something about
studying and had come right out and said he was going to be
busy both days. She was sure he hadn't mentioned any big test
coming up. Besides, he was always able to get everything done
in study hall anyway. Those annoying standardized tests weren't
scheduled until January, and their review class wasn't until the
seventeenth.

Monday couldn't come fast enough, and she started her day
out like any other. With her morning schedule on the other
end of the school, she still hadn't seen Will yet. Classes kept her
busy until their shared lunch time when her stomach reminded
her she needed a "food and Will" fix. It was always a good
combination. She was usually feeling very empty of both by

the afternoon. It was a great picker-upper that lasted until just before the end of school when she started craving her part-time job. At least for one day out of the reduced winter work week, anyway. She had recently convinced Mr. Jacobs to let her and Will both work together one evening. The timing couldn't have been better. She needed some one-on-one without family hovering over them.

"Hi Jenna, comment était votre week-end?" Tina asked, setting down her tray. She slid onto the bench and sat closer to Toby to make room for Jenna. Her friends were both wearing the same colors. Tina had on a brown sweater over her blue waffle-weave shirt. Toby was wearing a brown jersey with Property of Orchard Creek Football printed in turquoise blue. Tina looked from Toby's shirt to her own outfit and snorted a tiny laugh. Jenna hadn't gotten her lunch yet as she was late, having waited for Will. He wasn't outside his History room. Mr. Bosely said Will had just gotten up and left about five minutes before class ended, so Jenna waited. She expected him to return, but when the bell range four minutes later, her hope vanished with the resonating sound in the empty hallway. At any other time, she would have worried that he wasn't feeling well. Somehow, she knew it had nothing to do with his health.

Jenna replied to Tina's question in French without looking at her friend. "My weekend was lonely." She watched the Social Studies wing that emptied into the cafeteria. "Have you seen Will? He seems to be dodging me."

"What happened?" Toby asked, leaning forward on the table with both his large forearms.

"Remember the man's face I've been telling you both about?"

Tina and Toby nodded, now with growing interest.

"Well, I saw it again right before ceremony at Will's house, but this time, it started as a reflection in the mirror in Will's room. When I turned my head, it was like he was really there on Will's bed. When I turned back, there was no one there in the bedroom at all."

"His bedroom, huh?" Toby grinned.

"Shut up you idiot!" Tina shoved Toby in the arm but he barely moved. "Did you tell him about all the others times?" Tears started to well up in Jenna's eyes.

"Sorry, couldn't help myself. Sorry Jenna, really," Toby apologized earnestly, the smile gone.

"What did he say? He believed you, right?" Tina urged, her blue eyes staring at Jenna over her glasses. She became angry at Jenna's silence.

Tina's words were exactly what Jenna was worried about most. Even though Will had seen the face too, she was becoming paranoid he would think she was too weird for him. Unable to speak, Jenna nodded once, getting a hold of herself. "I told him and he seemed okay with it, but then it happened again during ceremony. Someone blew my candle out and the smoke made an outline of the man's face. Everyone could see it."

"What did they say?" Tina asked.

"They hadn't seen anything like that before. They tried to reassure me everything would be okay. I'm more worried that Will won't think I'm not worth the time. Lately, trouble is never far from me, and now I'm causing it at his own home."

"What were his exact words when you talked to him about it?" Toby asked, half way through his lunch now.

Jenna shook her head. "We were too busy dissecting every-thing with his family afterwards to have time to ourselves to talk about it. He blew me off all weekend, and now he left class early just to avoid me," She took in a huge shaky breath and blew it out noisily.

"You sound very sure he is avoiding you," Tina observed. Jenna kept her head down as she fiddled with the tie on her hoodie. "I'm sure there's a perfectly good explanation."

"You're both working tonight, right?" asked Toby, a plan forming. Jenna nodded again. "I'll come, too, and you can ask him then, okay? If he doesn't give you the answer you're looking for, I'll ask him my own questions."

Jenna nodded weakly through blurred vision.

It seemed to take forever until she drove into the museum parking lot. She had given herself a pep-talk driving over, but now the butterflies in her stomach pounded her trying to get loose. She felt like running, too, because Will's car wasn't here, and he was never late. She noticed Toby's truck parked at the end. Even though his house was practically next to the museum, it was too snowy to walk over. Having him there helped her to relax. She pulled her hood over her head, tucking her hair behind it awkwardly with her mittens.

Jenna knew this day was just getting better and better when she walked in and saw the expression on Toby's face. "He's not coming in tonight, is he?" she asked. Toby's grave expression answered her before he shook his head from side to side.

"Sulis was a bit curt with me, too," Toby admitted.

"You called his house?"

"I was curious. He's not feeling well or something, she

said," Toby stated. "I'll tell you what, it's going to be a slow night because of the weather. I can cover for you here. My dad won't mind. Why don't you take a ride over there and find out? It'll put your mind at ease. I know you, it'll eat you up otherwise, Jenna."

He was right. She was fast becoming a basket case. The rational part of her brain tried to reason that maybe he was sick. It was quickly overruled by her feelings of self-consciousness. Better to find out now he thought she was too psychically high maintenance before she put any more energy into worrying about it. She thanked Toby and walked back out into the blowing snow.

The short ride took much longer with the visibility nearly gone. If she hadn't known the roads so well, she would have careened off into the ditch in several places. The wind whipped across her windshield causing complete whiteouts at times. Once she thought she saw the man's face in the white flurries, but shrugged it off as nerves. Driving in bad weather was way down on her list of favorites.

She finally reached Will's house, parked the car and trudged through the foot-high drifts to the front door. She rang the doorbell three times before it was answered. She wasn't surprised to see Sulis's silhouette. Sulis opened the door slightly, obviously not an invitation to come in and stay.

"Oh, hi Jenna. Will isn't feeling well tonight. I thought Toby would have passed that on." Sulis looked the same as she usually did, wearing a matching tee shirt and stretch pants outfit. Her eyes seemed flatter, though, distant. There was no friendliness in them.

Jenna tried to peer around the large woman without looking like a stalker but couldn't. "Yeah, I got the message. I haven't talked to him since Friday night," she said firmly. "I thought I'd see if there was anything I could do." Jenna ran out of steam, her voice cracked at the end.

Sulis's expression softened, but it didn't touch her eyes. "I don't think so, honey. He's downstairs working on a project of some sort."

Just then, Will rounded the corner by the stairs and stopped abruptly. He stared at Jenna without any expression at all. Then, slowly, his face turned up in the mischievous smile she disliked. Just as Jenna was about to become angry at him, it morphed into a smile she hadn't seen before. She suddenly felt colder. Will stood there for a moment longer, without saying a word. The odd smile remained as he turned around and walked away.

"I'm sorry, Jenna. I can't invite you in tonight," Sulis said as she started to close the door. The door latched, and the silhouette disappeared before Jenna could reply. Sulis had never acted like that towards her before, and Jenna was confused. A half an inch of snow accumulated on her hood as she stood there. Somehow everything had changed and she tried to fight the thoughts that screamed she was the reason. She couldn't convince herself that Will really was sick with Sulis treating her that way. Her first instinct must have been right after all.

She turned around slowly and got back in her car to head for the museum. She felt like going home and wallowing in her room, but there was no way she wanted to be there after this with her family asking questions. Peter wouldn't really care why she looked so sad, but her mother or father would.

She hoped Toby was still there. An elusive thought nagged at her. Something was not right with this picture, she thought, something more than just a disgruntled boyfriend.

Toby was there, waiting for her at the main entrance. He opened the door with a frown on his face as she labored in. She looked like the covered object from the middle of a snow globe. She pulled her hood back and cakes of snow plopped onto the dark gray industrial rug.

"That was way too quick for an explanation," observed Toby, studying her. "You don't look relieved, either."

"She said he was sick, right to my face. He didn't look sick when he walked by the door."

Toby had taken Jenna's coat and led her to the bottom step of the staircase where she sat down. He sat next to her. His frown hadn't changed. "What did he say for himself?"

"He just gave me that stupid smile he gets when he's up to no good…oh!" Jenna suddenly remembered. Toby waited, not following.

"Will gets this certain smile on his face when he's doing something he's not supposed to. It was on his face when he had first used the Ouija board and left it open, and then when he tried to keep the hidden diamonds a secret. It's the exact same one I saw when he found Sylvia's athame at the end of Halloween night," Jenna continued on before realizing Toby wasn't privy to that information.

"What?" Toby asked, confused. "Sylvia's athame disappeared from the window after we did the spell outside."

"Yes, it did," Jenna's face began to redden, matching her cold cheeks. "After we all came back inside, Will and I went to put things away up in the loft, and Sylvia's athame was sitting on her altar. So, he took it." It hadn't seemed like such an awful thing to do at the time, but now that she thought about it from a different angle, she had second thoughts.

"Whoa, nobody said anything about that."

Jenna hung her head. "Nobody knows except us. He asked me not to tell anyone. Why do I listen to him? He promised he would put it away somewhere."

Toby started to shift uncomfortably. "What do you think he's doing now, using it? Do you think he conjured up that man?"

"I don't know. I think I started it because I've seen the face, not him. I've seen it once here, in the street, on my homework, in the library and, it sounds silly, but I swear I've seen it in the swirl the cream made that I put in my tea."

"Maybe he's seen it, too, and just hadn't said anything," Toby countered.

Jenna shrugged and continued. "Then there's the three times I've seen it at his house." She thought a moment. "Actually, each time I've been there I've seen it."

"Something is definitely stronger there. If he's using that thing in his house, we are all in trouble. Even Sulis admitted she doesn't understand what it's capable of. It's too dangerous. You've got to get it back."

"Maybe I should tell Sulis," she thought out loud to herself. "Yeah, I probably should. It wouldn't be the first time his confidence came with a price. I don't even know where he put it; his house is huge. There are so many cubbies and places..." Jenna trailed off. Toby put his arm around her and the smell of his cologne comforted her.

"It all started in his attic. I fell through this partition into a room they weren't aware of. It had some freaky things there, and that's when I first saw it. His aunts thought maybe the room was used during the Underground Railroad. Maybe I disturbed a spirit, and now it's following me."

"Freaky, huh? That doesn't explain why Will is acting so strange, though."

"No, it doesn't. Maybe he's trying to protect me. Maybe he's trying to use the athame to get rid of the man himself," Jenna suggested half-heartedly. She was just about to describe the freaky things from the attic when they were interrupted.

"Hey!" Toby yelled. They both jumped when they heard a noise below them that turned into a loud whine. The power shut off abruptly.

"Tobe, can you check that out?" Mr. Jacobs yelled from the office. "And make sure the generator goes on so I can run the backup in here or I'll lose all my records."

"Sure! Jenna and I are on it! Come help me find the flash-lights." Toby stood and shuffled slowly.

"Um, there's one by the desk and one by the main door. I think I can get to the door," Jenna said, her voice drifting further away. It was quiet without the steady hum from the lights they were used to hearing. Now and then she heard a thump followed by an expletive as Toby ran into things. At almost the same time, two clicks sounded and beams of light flashed from opposite ends of the room.

"Why isn't the generator picking this up already?" Toby

asked aloud. They reached each other and started down the steep steps to the basement. "Dad, where are the instructions for the genny?"

His father answered at the same time Jenna did. "In the corner of the basement."

"I think all the paperwork for it is locked in the electrical cabinet on the southern side," Jenna remembered, leading the way. "I haven't used it in years, but the key should be hanging up right on the side of the cabinet."

They reached the bottom of the stairs and started towards the generator, Toby joking about security when the lights suddenly flickered on. For an instant, a full-sized image of the man appeared directly in front of them, outlined in white light like the afterglow of a bright bulb. The lights cut out again, and Jenna felt Toby react. He swung his flashlight towards the figure, but Jenna was too close and his flashlight hit the top of her head with a dull thud. Her flashlight fell to the floor and she dropped into a sitting position just as the lights brightened to full power. The man was gone. They were the only ones in the room.

"What was that? Was that the figure you've been seeing? Oh, Jenna, sorry. Are you okay?"

"Bell!" Jenna heard herself say. She sat there a second longer, rubbing her head.

"Did you just swear? You never swear. Sorry! Let me take a look," Toby said kneeling next to her.

"Yeah, that's the man. And no, I said "bell," Toby. Why did I say bell?" she asked, as Toby's large hands felt along her head.

"Huh. I don't know. You're still in one piece, though. It

didn't break the skin, but you'll probably have a lump." He helped her up and they scanned the empty basement. Jenna brushed her bottom off as she looked at Toby expectantly.

"Well, now I've seen him, too. What do we do?"

"I was hoping you would have an answer. I guess I've got to talk to Will."

Nine

THE RINGING IN her ears woke her up only a minute before the radio alarm went off. School was closed due to the inclement weather, the DJ announced. Approaching Will in school had been her first plan of attack, but this was even better. She would manage through the nor'easter to his house herself and corner him there.

It wasn't something her parents would condone. If the roads weren't good enough for parochial transit, she was sure, according to them, it wouldn't be good enough for her and her Chevy Cavalier. She weighed her options. She was determined to talk to him face to face today. It was too far to walk, probably even more dangerous. She had all day to do this. The ride there and back, taking her time and being careful, along with the intervention would have her back home before dinner time with no harm done.

She could call Toby if she really needed to, but his strategy wouldn't be conducive to getting the information she needed as much as giving physical opinions. He was such a big brother. Her plans were still fuzzy on what to do when she confronted Will, but she had enough to start with. Jenna sighed as she took out a turtleneck sweater and a hoodie.

An hour later she pulled into the snow-blown driveway and shut off the engine. Her stomach was still churning from the slippery drive, and now it was just as upset when she looked at the house. As she walked up to the door, she saw a curtain in the living room move aside.

"Hi Jenna, come in please," Will offered when he answered the door. Jenna entered the house, keeping her eye on Will. He was dressed in green khakis and a long sleeve shirt. His hair was pulled back into a ponytail. The clothes and color choices were predictable for Will, the ponytail was not. He didn't apologize for the night before, or offer any explanation.

"For what do I owe this visit?" he asked. The formality of the greeting reminded Jenna of manners of long ago. Mrs. Forrester was the first person who popped into her mind.

"Are you mad at me, Will?" she began. Something about the lack of expression on his face made her nervous. Usually, he smiled when he saw her, especially after a weekend apart. His face looked different; his eyes were tighter. She certainly didn't like the ponytail thing. It didn't look like Will at all.

"No, of course not." At his side, his thumb started to rub across his first finger.

"I haven't seen you, or talked to you since Friday night. That's an unusually long time for us to go without talking."

Just then, Rommy ran into the room towards Jenna. Will

bent down to call him over, but the cat stopped and stared at him, his fur rising along his back. Instead of coming closer, he looked up at Jenna and meowed loudly. Will's hand stopped twitching and he sighed. It made him look sad. "I've been feeling a little sick, and I didn't want you to catch anything. Anyway, I've been doing some research."

"Oh," Jenna replied. She was caught off guard and at a loss to say anything else. Was it really as simple as a bad cold? If that was the case, she had wasted too much time and energy stressing for nothing.

"Forgive me, please. I had no intention to worry you." The soft-spoken tone was back where it belonged. The stomach twinged and she forgave him before the words were out.

"Come. I want to show you what I've learned." When she had peeled away several outer layers, Will offered her his hand. She noted he had several cuts across his knuckles and inside web of his palm that had just started to scab over. She was surprised when they didn't go upstairs towards the attic. Instead, he led her downstairs to the canning cellar.

Jenna hesitantly wedged into the nook when he motioned for her to walk in. Will put his arm around her, and she had to fight off the urge to wiggle herself out and run away. Even his cologne didn't affect her the same way as it had before. She couldn't explain why she felt so on edge.

Will clicked on the flashlight and a strong light shown from over her head, illuminating the board much better than the first time she had seen it. Carvings into the wood covered the top and down the right side of the slab. The arrangement reminded her of the squares of a board game and the carvings looked like simplistic letters. She remembered seeing them on the scary knife, too, but it was all Greek to her. This she kept to herself, only nodding in forced interest.

"I've been looking into that wooden board in the corner and all those markings. They're runes."

Jenna nodded again. "Wow." That history was a little too historic for her. She didn't know what to make of it. Her eyes were drawn to the scratches and gashes instead. Most were old and weathered except in certain areas. The ends of the wood where it fit into the wall and some of the empty knots had new dig marks. She was sure they were new because they had rough edges and the coloring was lighter than the rest of the wood.

"Why does this—?" she started to say as she reached out to touch one of the holes. The light moved away quickly and Will maneuvered himself into her field of vision.

"You are amazing, do you know that? You could be so helpful to me. I've missed you the last few days. I'm sorry it felt like you were overlooked. There's so much here to learn and we do make such a good team. We could work together, don't you think?" Abruptly, he pushed past her, knocking her into the side of the wall. She walked out slowly, her brow furrowed.

"So many pieces to put together. Do you think of anything particular when you're down here? Your talent certainly has to have left you with some remnant of its history other than that man." Will waited.

Jenna wanted to break away from the uncomfortable stare. She shook her head slowly. Her thoughts actually did center on something particular more than once, but she didn't feel she should share it with Will. Something was off. He didn't look at her the same way, and she didn't feel attracted to him like she did before. Right now, he was giving her the creeps.

"Oh, come now. You've been inside Amelie's head which was shared with Sylvia."

"What does Sylvia have to do with your house?" Jenna mumbled, her heart starting to race.

Will nodded nonchalantly. "Oh, I'm sure a lot more than we know. I did find a date in that cubby that is in the same time frame as the Boarding House. After all, the pictures we found down here were of her and the building."

"Have you seen the man here anymore? Who do you think he is?" she found herself asking.

Will chuckled. The sound of it was foreign to Jenna. "No, I haven't seen him. All is well. The information I located with that date was of a man named Karl Gruen. He lived here with his daughter, Elsa."

"Elsa," she parroted back without thinking. She didn't seem to be able to break away from his eyes. His gaze was more like looking through her and her thoughts were getting jumbled in her head. She managed to get out the one question she really needed to know. "What does your mom think about all of this?"

His expression changed just a fraction before he looked away. The set of his face hardened. "She hasn't found out as much as I have."

Jenna knew that was probably the most honest thing he said to her today. "Maybe we should ask her…" she goaded.

"You can try." Will smiled at her innocently. The tone of his voice suggested he was teasing as much as he was taunting, and with the look on his face, it made the hair on her neck stand up.

Sulis didn't have an inkling of what he was up to. Jenna intended to change that as soon as possible, and she needed to tell Toby everything. He was rational. Was something really different about Will? Maybe he could figure out if she was losing her mind. Will had said nothing to her that would cause the fear she felt now.

She slowly made her way out of the cellar, explaining about having to go home and do chores. Will followed calmly behind her, pacing himself the way a hunter might follow its prey. His eyes were locked on her but they never seemed to blink, and his face held an expression she had never seen before. It made her feel as if she was being stalked. She wanted out, out of the house, and away from Will. She pulled on her coat, hat and scarf as quickly as she could without looking obvious. She pecked Will on the check and did her best to smile. He closed the door saying he would see her in school tomorrow. The snow had stopped, the brightness blinding her until her eyes adjusted. A neighboring dog was barking loudly in the distance, muffling the laughter Jenna swore she heard behind the closed door that was very unlike Will's.

Jenna didn't waste time before she was on the phone. It rang several times as she dropped her winter gear throughout the house, trying to find what she was looking for.

"You have reached Rebekah Greenley..." the message began.

"Dang, not good. Hi Sulis, it's Jenna. Hey, I have something kind of important to ask you. Please give me a call back at home, any time, okay? It's important and concerns Will's safety. Thanks."

Jenna hung the phone back in the cradle and sat down to think. She picked the phone back up but put it down again. In the kitchen she found the phonebook and flipped through the pages until she came across the name she was looking for. She hoped she had spelled it correctly, there were too many listed to try each one.

It was just getting dark when she finally put the phone down for good. Shaking her head as if trying to dislodge water from her ear from swimming, she tried to yawn to clear the ringing from her ears. She was also getting hoarse and went to make some hot tea. Her parents weren't due to get home from work until just before dinner. Peter had been holed up in his room most of the afternoon, enjoying the luxury of no homework, and the never-ending excitement of video games. She had excitement all right.

"Forget the videos; mine are the interactive type," she said sourly. She was thinking of how she was going to go forward. Her strategy was flimsy. That uneasy feeling came back when she thought of Will. He had crossed the line that was for sure. The hot water stopped whistling as soon as it left the burner. Jenna started to pour it into her teacup when there was a loud knock at the door, startling her out of her rumination. The pot jerked, splashing the boiling water over her right hand, scalding her.

"Peter!" Jenna yelled to the bedroom. No one answered. "Headsets should be outlawed," she griped to herself, as she cranked the faucet handle. The cool water from the sink numbed the pain, but when the water was turned off, the heat came back. The knock was now growing impatient. Jenna wrapped her hand in a wet towel and ran for the door. Her hand was the least of her worries two seconds later.

SULIS LISTENED TO her messages. Several were work related, one was an optical appointment reminder, and one she had no idea what to do about. What could Jenna possibly need from her? She hadn't really made up her mind about all that. It would have to wait. She had two readings to do later, squeeze in dinner, and then she had to look for something. For a split second Sulis couldn't remember what it was she had to look for, only that the urge had scratched annoyingly in her head all afternoon. It caught up to her, and the urge subsided. Of course that was it, how could she forget?

The paper she picked up from her desk began to distract her from the evening's chores. Only a few more hours at work. She was hoping she would be able to sleep better tonight. She was dragging, yawning every five minutes or so. The caffeine overload she had used to compensate for her fatigue had backfired. She would be here later than she wanted. She had only been able to work sporadically, stopping so often to visit the ladies' room. Well, she wasn't a spring chicken anymore.

At least the snow had stopped and her ride home would be easier than the ride in. That was one of the good things about Central New York. A blizzard could incapacitate the whole area for the morning commute and be completely plowed away and cleared by rush-hour home. Her thoughts drifted to the time crunch between getting home and the readings she loved so much. Jenna's phone call was completely forgotten.

Ten

*J*ENNA FUMBLED WITH the lock with her good hand. The door opened with a flourish as she slipped in the melted snow on the tile and caught herself at the last minute. There, in front of her was Will. He stood quietly as she slid and steadied herself.

"Oh, ow, ugh, my hand!" Jenna had grabbed the door jamb with her towel, leaking more water on the already slick floor. She would have caught herself sooner but she was surprised, and somewhat scared, to see Will standing there.

"Hi, Jenna. What have you been doing? I tried to call for over an hour, and the line was busy."

Several thoughts crossed her mind simultaneously. Why was it the fact that he couldn't reach her the most important thing he was concerned with at the moment? Was Sulis all right? He didn't look upset at all for it to be an emergency. Why was he so nosy about what she was doing, anyway?

"I was on the phone, obviously," she answered tersely. The pain in her hand and the unanswered questions in her head had her defensive and edgy.

"Aren't you going to invite me in? It is cold out here."

Jenna looked towards the bedrooms quickly and nodded. She was hesitant to have him come inside, not because her parents weren't home, although that was the house rule. She was more concerned with the fact that Peter couldn't hear anything from his room.

Will walked in slowly. "With whom?" he asked casually, slipping off his boots and walking in the direction of the living room.

"Huh? What?" Jenna stammered, watching him as he went further into her home. She followed behind tentatively, trying to find a way to lead him back to the door.

"Who were you on the phone with for so long?" he asked sharply as he sat on the couch. His mouth turned up in a smile that didn't touch his eyes. He patted the cushion next to him for her to sit down.

Jenna certainly did not want to sit next to him. How she could get him out of her house? He didn't look like he would listen if she reminded him of her parents' rule. There was no easy way and that fact made her realize she was stuck. Shaking her head "no," she motioned to her wrapped, still dripping hand as to the reason why she wasn't sitting. Will looked at her hand with a blank stare and nodded his head once, acknowledging.

"Uh, I was going over some business with Toby for the museum for a while. If you'll excuse me, I have to..."

"Oh. I wasn't aware of anything new happening," he interrupted, settling himself into the seat. "Tell me about it."

"Look, Will. I don't want you to get into trouble being here…" Jenna held her arm to her chest and covered it with her good hand. The cooled water seeped into her shirt, chilling her. Goosebumps began to cover her body. Her stomach was tightening in a very uncomfortable way and there was a ringing in her ears again.

Will tilted his head to the side once and effortlessly rose from the couch. Slowly and silently he walked back to the kitchen. When their eyes met, it appeared he was still waiting for an answer. Jenna tried to look at everything from an outsider's perspective, but couldn't really see anything out of the ordinary. She wasn't very good at lying, but every fiber of her being seemed to want to keep all her thoughts to herself. And especially her internal emotions. Will had once said he didn't like to "eavesdrop" on what other people were feeling because it felt intrusive. She crossed her fingers he had his empathic wall up. She grabbed the first idea that came to her.

"Well, there's the loft. I think we might want to open that up to the public. Of course, we'd need to clean up Sylvia's altar and all the things on it."

Will's flat expression lifted. "Really? Why, that would be grand. I'll have to let Mr. Jacobs know I'll be available to work with you on that project straight away."

"What about Sylvia's athame?" Jenna blurted out. Her breathing had sped up, and she tried to hide how obvious it was by walking over to the sink.

"No. We agreed it was going to be put away," Will countered, still following her.

"Is it put away, Will?" Jenna asked, looking down at the porcelain. She concentrated on re-soaking the warm, wet towel in cold water. Her hand was red and sore but not blistering. Will watched her face, patiently. When she couldn't avoid it any longer, she looked up, searching his eyes.

"Yes, it is. I haven't touched it," he said sincerely. His deep brown eyes bore into hers, making her thoughts fragment and scatter like bugs when a light is turned on. "Is that why you've been uneasy around me? I made you a promise, didn't I? Don't you trust me?"

"Sure I do," Jenna found herself answering. Something told her to fake it and fake it good. That too much rested on this. She smiled and consciously relaxed her tense shoulders. Reaching up to him, Jenna ran her good hand through his long hair, the ponytail gone now. Her fingers got tangled in a necklace he was wearing on a thin black rope that had a jagged black stone on the end. She looked up at him and smiled to divert his attention from her discovery. She hadn't known Will to ever have worn it before.

"I trust you with my heart and soul."

Will smiled, distracted, hugging her tightly. "I'm so happy to hear that."

"Will, why did you come over?"

"I had a bad feeling, is all." He continued to hold her although the hug had ended and now it just felt like being bound. "I suppose I should go so you don't get into trouble with me here. Let's try to get together soon, to talk more, okay?

I'd like to know what your thoughts are about things, what you think of, what you dream about, everything."

He kissed her on the cheek and walked out the door without looking back. Jenna stood there for a minute watching him get back into his car. She smiled and waved before she dashed to the bathroom. She made it just in time to throw up.

Jenna had composed herself just as her parents came home. They usually arrived within a few minutes of each other, and fortunately, neither had run into Will. She was frustrated, though. She wanted to call Sulis at work and at home, hoping to reach her before Will returned, but had run out of time.

Peter emerged from his cave almost a half an hour later, unaware of Will ever having been over. Jenna ate just enough to settle her tender stomach, excusing herself to her room for the night. She was glad now she had made her earlier phone calls. She wasn't going to second-guess herself anymore. If anything, she was going to go with her gut feeling. Something was up and something was definitely not right.

Climbing into bed at 8:30 wasn't her usual style, although Jenna always went to bed early. She was exhausted for some reason, and fell into a deep sleep almost immediately. She woke up a short time later, gasping. It had been one of those dreams where she was paralyzed, but aware of everything around her. There were too many strange things that didn't make sense. She didn't understand what was happening to her and tried to sort out the dream to flesh out the reason the bell seemed so important that it repeated over and over. Not necessarily in her dreams. She had yelled it out in the basement of the museum with Toby, and had heard it in her head so much since the day before that she thought she had somehow damaged her ears. Then there was something Will wanted from her, only her. A bell seemed innocuous enough. Could that be what he was after? He certainly was interested in finding out. She didn't know the significance of it, but something very persistently told her to keep the thoughts of the bell away from him. Whatever Jenna was receiving was something Sylvia must have had knowledge of. Was Sylvia giving her clues? And why hadn't Sulis called? She needed to get her alone, to talk to her.

Jenna tried putting the pieces of this puzzle together but couldn't make it fit; her mind was not working properly with so little sleep. She looked up at the pitch-black ceiling, listening to the quiet in the house. Turning her bedside light on, she was momentarily blinded by the bright light. She opened the drawer in the nightstand and pulled out paper, making too much noise looking for a pen. She could only find a marker, but it would do. She quickly wrote down all the things that had been bothering her.

Was I the one who conjured the man?

Who is he and why does he keep appearing?

Why does a bell keep repeating in my head?

Why do Will and Sulis both seem to be acting strangely?

What does Will want from me?

How exactly has Will changed that makes me nervous?

Does Sylvia's athame have anything to do with it?

What is up with Will's necklace?

Why is the cellar nook weird?

She was surprised to see how much of the paper was written on when she was done. She skimmed over it, looking for something obvious, but nothing jumped out at her. The clock read just past midnight and she was tired. It was too late do anything about it right now. Clicking the light, Jenna fell back on her pillow expecting sleep to come quickly, but it was a long time before she finally drifted off. She was unable to discern sleeping from the twilight state she was in for four hours, staring at the ceiling.

THE NEXT DAY was Wednesday, December seventh. Jenna plopped her tray at the table and slid onto the bench, bumping ungracefully into Toby. He was the first one to make it through the lunch line, as usual, and was already half-way through his greasy pizza.

"You look awful, Jenna," he commented. Jenna picked at her food, but was too busy holding her head up with her hand to really want to eat. "Are you sure you still want to come over to the museum tonight?" he asked.

"Yeah, I do. Darn, I forgot to bring the list I was making. I'll have to stop at home first to get it." Jenna yawned hugely. "It shouldn't take me longer than a half an hour."

Will sat down next to Jenna at the same time Tina joined them. Jenna stiffened in her seat, still yawning. Will looked at her, amused.

"Not getting enough sleep? What's bothering you?"

Jenna just shook her head, shrugging it off.

"Don't worry, I'm here to protect you," Will reassured her. Jenna stopped mid-yawn, her mouth snapping shut, finally wide awake now.

"Nope. Sleeping like a baby, just went to bed too late, I guess." Jenna turned toward Toby trying to make eye contact with him.

Toby stopped chewing as he looked from Jenna to Will. Nodding, he looked down as if he dropped a piece of pepperoni. Jenna wanted to tell Toby she had made another call at Sulis's work number before she left the house that morning, and how she hoped she would get a call back at home later, but she couldn't say more. It would be a long afternoon.

A few hours later Jenna was home. She squeezed out of her boots at the door, her hands full with the mail and her book bag. She looked over at the answering machine on the breakfast island. No messages. Sulis hadn't called her back. Again. Jenna frowned, thinking how odd that seemed to her. Sulis always acted like she was available if it was something important.

The book bag started to slide out of her arms and down her leg. Jenna nudged it to the floor with her foot like a hacky sack. She dropped the pile of mail and threw her car keys onto the oak dining room table just outside the kitchen. They slid across its length just missing the wooden sleigh centerpiece filled with peppermints, and tumbled onto a chair as she continued to walk toward her room.

Her goal was to get her list and be on her way. She was sidetracked as she looked down at the assortment of Christmas cards and bills splayed on the table. Among them was a small, slender package, about the size of a watch box, addressed to her. It was simply wrapped in brown paper with no return address. Hesitantly taking the box, she opened it, wondering in the back of her mind if she should. It was a jewelry box and inside was a modest, sturdy silver chain. On it, wound tightly by a fine silver band that offered a loop to be strung on the chain, was an amethyst stone just a little smaller than the size of a jawbreaker. It was smooth, not completely round, with dark violet and plum facets interspersed with clear sections.

"Huh," she said out loud to the house. Peter had intramurals for the next three hours. Was this a Christmas present? Her birthday was in February, and the variegated, purple-hued crystal was her birthstone. It took her a second to think about looking for a note. Tucked under the cotton was a small piece of stationery.

"'Wear this and don't take it off.' That's it? What the..." Jenna had turned the paper over but found no other instructions or who sent it. The necklace was shiny and very beautiful. Jenna walked toward her room, latching the chain under her thick hair, smiling when it hung by her cleavage where she could admire the stone when she looked down. Something about it made her feel good and she smiled. She thought about the possible senders as she smoothed the stone against her chest and reached for her list.

Her hand froze and her heart beat so loudly she could feel it in her temples. The list was there on her night stand. The page was now filled in, her neat penmanship written in marker. The bottom third wasn't part of her list; it was lines of words that rhymed ending with a bunch of letters grouped together. The rhyming words repeated over and over.

Laura Livingston Snyder

Bell tell hell door more store Dual Yule fuel Find mind bind
Bell tell hell door more store Dual Yule fuel Find mind bind
Bell tell hell door more store Dual Yule fuel Find mind bind

BRRS   APG
EEIK   WSNY

116

Eleven

*T*HE WHOLE PAGE was filled, yet Jenna couldn't remember writing it. "What the heck is this?" Her voice trembled meekly in the silence. She couldn't make her brain recall when she had penned it, no matter how hard she tried. The phone rang and a shrill screech escaped her lips. She jumped up, blocking the nightstand. Clutching the paper, it crinkled in her rush to fold it. She jammed it into her pocket and impatiently brushed a loose strand of hair away from her face. She should have felt silly hiding paper from a ringing phone, but Jenna couldn't help but feel she was being watched.

"Huh, hello?"

"Good afternoon! What's new?" Will's chipper voice asked on the other end.

Jenna had trouble finding enough air to talk. "Not much, just came inside. I need to catch my breath a sec."

"Oh. Would you like some company tonight? Mom has readings, and I'm sure I'll be bored. I'd rather spend time with you, if you don't mind."

Jenna's mind raced with excuses. For some reason, her stomach soured with the idea that Will had sent her the necklace. She fingered it, soothed by its coolness.

"Sorry. I think both my parents are working late tonight. Holidays coming up, you know?"

"No worries. By the way, you will be over for Yule, right? It's going to be at our house on the twenty-first. We have a lot scheduled and it will be a great ceremony."

"My plans haven't changed. I'm looking forward to it. Everyone will be there?" asked Jenna.

"They certainly will."

"Hey, I'll see you tomorrow in school, 'kay?" Jenna hung up the phone. She knew she only had a few hours to get to the museum and make it back home in case he called again. She patted her pocket and the list crunched in confirmation. She turned to the door when the phone rang for a second time. She jumped once more; looking briefly out the window, just to be sure Will wasn't outside. It was irrational, but it put her mind at ease to only see her car out front. The greeting at the other end made Jenna relax. It was Toby.

"I thought you were on your way?"

"Temporary interruption. Toby, I don't think my house or phone is safe anymore."

"You're getting paranoid. Come right over then; I'm by myself except for my dad."

"Toby, I know this is overkill, but if I'm not there in seven minutes, come looking for me, okay?" she pleaded.

"You'll be fine, just get here," Toby told her.

The ride over was uneventful. She parked on the other side of Toby's usual spot with some effort. He always picked the end. At least her car was obscured by his pickup truck. She kept looking over her shoulder on the way inside.

"I am losing my mind," she grumbled under her breath. Toby met her at the door, and she hugged him, needing reassurance of safety. His navy cotton tee was soft and smelled of Oleg Cassini cologne. It was what Toby had smelled like for years. A hollow feeling in the pit of her stomach reminded her it used to be Will she sought out for that comfort.

"I think I need to make this quick. Will called me just before you did. I received this in the mail, and then he calls and asks me what's new." Jenna cradled the stone in her hand for him to see.

"Hmm," he answered, unimpressed. "A lot of people ask that when they're on the phone, you know." When his attempt to lighten the mood failed, he changed gears. "You think he mailed this to you? Why would he mail it? This is messing with your head. Come on." He pulled her forward to the office where Mr. Jacobs was waiting.

After an hour of recapping her story, Jenna was tired again. Mr. Jacobs hardly spoke at all but was deep in thought. Toby leaned into the file cabinet with his beefy arms across his chest, watching them both.

"I don't understand the extra words on your paper, Jenna," Mr. Jacobs admitted.

"I don't either. Whatever fragments were floating in her head were maybe put there by someone other than her. This puzzle's a challenge I'd like to take up," Toby offered.

"Where do you think they came from?" Mr. Jacobs asked, ignoring his son.

"I wish I knew. It's scary, seeing something you've obviously written when you can't remember doing. Is there anything else I've done that I don't remember? Man, I'd love to speak to Sulis about all of this, but she won't return any of my calls."

"Yeah, Toby's mentioned that too. Are they working together on something?"

That took Jenna by surprise. It never crossed her mind. She shook her head because it didn't feel right. "She wouldn't, I'm sure. There's nothing that would benefit her."

"It's a new challenge. She even said it was way beyond what she was capable of."

"I just have a bad feeling about everything. That knife Will found looked... well, it looked evil. It had spiders and skulls and weird writing on it. Who knows who or what's been killed with that thing?"

A low grumble shook the room just as the lights flickered and dimmed.

"What is the problem with the electric now? The power has been going out quite a bit and the generator is not helping. That dumb thing has been temperamental for over a week. Where is that maintenance number?" Mr. Jacobs muttered as he pushed his chair out, searching his folders. Jenna got up slowly, her head down, as if trying to figure something out.

"What is it?" Toby asked bending over to look at her face.

"Bell. It repeats more here. When the lights dimmed, that stupid bell started in my ears again. It's getting louder, too."

"Do you think someone is sending you messages?" Mr. Jacobs sat back down with an invoice, picking up the phone.

"I don't know. Maybe Sylvia if Will's playing around with her athame," Jenna suggested.

"Wait, you said it's getting louder here? The last time we were in the basement, the lights went out, too," Toby remembered. "Let's follow that, Jenna. If Sylvia is trying to protect us somehow, we need to follow it. What if there's a connection?"

Mr. Jacobs put the phone back on the cradle. He frowned. "If there's a connection between Sylvia and Jenna, there's a connection to Sulis, too."

"Wow, could Sulis be hearing a bell, too?" Jenna wondered aloud.

The three set off down the steep basement stairs.

"I don't recall seeing a bell in any of the pictures of the boarding house. If Sylvia used one to call the boarders for dinner, or whatever, it's long gone," Mr. Jacobs stated.

"Anyway, if it was still here in this building – and that's a big 'if'—we would have found it when we cleaned up. A bell would be too obvious to miss, right? Weren't those things huge?" Toby asked. Jenna was about to comment when the lights cut out completely. Fortunately, they had just stepped off the steps, so they didn't fall. It was unexpected, though, and they ran into each other anyway, reminding Toby of an old Three Stooges movie.

"I knew I should have brought the flashlight. Hold on," Toby's hands moved over his father and Jenna's head as he tried to make his way to the staircase. The sound of his boots scuffed higher and higher before growing fainter a level above.

Jenna shuddered. "Ooh, cold chill." It wasn't just being chilled on the inside. Jenna felt a rush of cold air by her face just as someone bumped into her much too closely. She backed up to get out of the way and was bumped into again, arms coming down against her arms. Her mouth felt like cotton as she realized it wasn't Mr. Jacobs.

"Stop it, get away from me!" Jenna yelled, swinging her arms to break away from the unseen person. She began to cry. Tears ran down her face as hands found her shoulder seconds before Toby stormed back down the stairs, the flashlight bobbing and shining on them both. Jenna curled her arms around herself, hugging tightly. The memory of being attacked by Seth Sawyer always put her over the edge. It was made worse by the fact that again it was not Will who held her. Her breath hitched, and she stopped herself from crying. When the light finally stopped on her, it showed Mr. Jacobs with one hand on Jenna's back, the other waving into the air as if searching for something tangible.

"What just happened?" Toby demanded. His father turned toward Toby, his face pale in the bright beam of light. Jenna looked petrified.

"Someone is down here with us," Mr. Jacobs replied, his voice raspy with anxiety. He hugged Jenna tightly as Toby swept the light back and forth. There was nothing out of the ordinary. Jenna sniffed and rubbed her nose with her sleeve, muttering about a man.

"Get the generator on, Tobe, so we can check the circuit

breaker. Maybe we blew a fuse. It's okay, Jenna, we're all here."
Jenna tried to take deep breaths as she watched Toby walk away.

Toby walked over to the box on the southern wall hesitantly, shining the flashlight back to allow the light to illuminate the others. He felt too far away to help if the vision of the man returned. Only now that vision had materialized into something more substantial. Toby had been in that situation before and no good could come of the past once it became physical here. Without intending to, he realized he had placed himself, Jenna, and his dad into the Good category, leaving Sulis and Will in the Evil. He wished this problem would just quit already. This stuff wasn't his arena.

Toby felt helpless without their assistance and even more badly for Jenna. He had known her too long to ignore how this was affecting her. He had been jealous at first to see her find someone special. He wasn't jealous of wanting that relationship with Jenna, he was envious of not having his own. She was so happy and she and Will complemented each other well; he was as psychically abnormal as she was. He did not think this in a malicious way, he wanted only the best for her because he considered her family. His mind wandered briefly as he wondered when he would meet someone who fit him just right. He reached his hand towards the side of the wooden electrical box that was as tall as a fire extinguisher and twice as wide.

The only sound besides Jenna's shaky breathing was the key on the side jingling and the metal sound of it finding its home. The light momentarily shown inside the electrical box as Toby gasped, his attention finally focusing. The light bounced upwards as he was taken off guard. "Whoa! Holy s—"

"What happened?" Jenna asked quickly from across the room. She broke free from

Mr. Jacobs and ran to join her friend. She searched the area the flashlight was aimed at. The light centered on the bottom corner of the electrical box. Tucked way into the back was a small tarnished bell.

"What would Sulis and Will say to me joining in this ceremony?" Mr. Jacobs asked quietly. They had made their way back to the small office of the museum. The lights were on and working fine now without any intervention. "I feel I have a responsibility here to make sure this is taken care of."

"Hold on just a minute. No one's having anything without me there. I'm a lot sturdier than any of you, you know." Toby puffed up just a bit.

"I guess it wouldn't hurt to ask. After all, we all were in this together before. You don't think he would get suspicious?"

"We have to be straightforward about this. We can't let any more time pass where it could get worse. You're hearing a bell and Will wants something from you. Have you been coerced by him to find this bell? Something or someone has. We don't know what it's for or who we are protecting it from."

Jenna nodded sullenly, looking at the four-inch bell in her hands. It looked plain enough, oxidized by time to a black-ish-gray color. The bell itself was small; only two inches or so tall and had a short crown on top, just the right size to pick up by hand to ring. It was heavy, cast iron, maybe. She started to get nervous.

"Mr. Jacobs, I can't bring this back home. It makes me feel very vulnerable to have this in my possession."

"I can keep it locked up in here." Mr. Jacobs reached over and took the bell by the curve, the clapper trying to do its job unsuccessfully. A file cabinet was opened and the bell disappeared inside. The drawer was locked, and the keys slid into his jacket.

Jenna said her goodbyes and headed out the door. She was constantly looking over her shoulder, afraid she'd see Will come up behind her, but he never did. No sooner did she get in the kitchen door, the phone rang.

"That's probably for me," Jenna said, her lips pursed as she began plucking off her winter garb.

Her father put the soup ladle down on the stove. He picked up the phone, answered, and then looked over at her, smiling.

"If Tom Jacobs hadn't called just a few minutes ago to let us know you were at work, I'd be thinking you were off with Will all this time." The phone was passed over without question.

"Hi Will, what's up?" Jenna asked without waiting for a greeting.

"My, you are intuitive," replied Will on the other end.

"I just had a feeling. You seem to know what I'm doing all the time now," Jenna stated.

A bright chuckle on the other end made Jenna shudder. "Now, how could I know that? I was just calling to give you the firmed-up time for Yule. We're aiming for six in the evening this Wednesday. I realize the extended vacation doesn't start until Friday. Does that conflict with any of your holiday plans?"

"No, that sounds great." Jenna thought about the word "conflict" and decided she most definitely felt conflicted. "By the way, I mentioned the Yule ceremony to Toby and Mr. Jacobs—"

"They are more than welcome to come, too," Will cut in abruptly. "The more the merrier. You will pass the invitation along to them, won't you?"

"Sure," Jenna agreed cautiously. "Thanks, Will. Good night." She hung the phone up slowly.

"You okay, Jenna? Did you and Will get into a fight? You hardly hang out with him anymore," her dad asked. They were the only ones in the room. She could hear her mother scolding Peter in the basement about balled-up socks. The sound of the washing machine being turned on muffled their voices.

"Yes, not really, no," Jenna answered both questions at once, feeling uncomfortable. "It's a long story. Mr. Jacobs didn't mention anything to you?"

Now it was her dad's turn to look uncomfortable. "Well, yeah, he did, actually. I was hoping you'd want to tell me yourself. Am I that un-cool that I can't be kept in the loop when it comes to that building, not to mention my only daughter?"

"No. Sorry, Dad. It didn't start out so bad. Somehow, it's gotten out of control," Jenna admitted, taking the wrinkled list from her pocket. She sat down on the stool at the kitchen counter and passed the paper across to her father. She gave him the highlights, knowing the rest of the family would be upstairs soon. He looked over the list muttering now and then.

"So, if Will's using Sylvia's athame, I think we're all a little nervous," she said once he was done reading. She swiveled side to side absentmindedly.

Mr. Stevens shook his head. "Forget Sylvia's athame. What about this skull knife? Can't that be used as an athame too?"

"No way, Dad, I—" The words got stuck in Jenna's throat as things clunked into place. It was a very long time before she could put all the possibilities flying around in her head in order. She had always thought of it as a knife, not an athame.

"That's dark magic, and you're right; Sulis wouldn't touch it. I may not know her very well, but what I do know of her," he shook his head, "she wouldn't do that."

Jenna's face was white. "Will touched it. Didn't Sulis say after Halloween that certain things could be a, uh…"

"Trigger object that could be used—"

"To attract the paranormal," Jenna finished, her hand automatically reaching up to caress the amethyst.

Twelve

THIS CONVERSATION REPLAYED itself over and over as Jenna tried to relax enough to sleep. Jenna had told her dad everything about the necklace. After his brief irritation with being left out of what he apparently felt was his parental obligation to voice his opinion, agreed she should keep it on. Once again she held her necklace, her fingers running over the smooth, polished stone. The note said not to take it off. She thought about it, but it felt *right* to keep it on, even though she did not know why.

With her hand still firmly holding the stone, she finally drifted off into an intense dream surrounded by everyone she had talked to that day. Sulis was there, too, but fuzzy and dark around the edges. Will was hard to focus on. Every time she looked at him there was a cloud of translucent black smoke obscuring him. The bell was ringing clearly, even though she could see it sitting on an altar. It was plain as day, illuminated by the shard of yellow-looking glass. Although nothing else was moving, the cloth covering the altar was swaying back and forth heavily.

Jenna moved around the loft at the museum, looking at Sylvia's altar from all directions. She felt there was something important she needed to see so her body relaxed and allowed that to happen. The bell and the light grew louder and brighter until they hurt both her ears and eyes. She raised her hand and a flash of white flew out of her fingertips, lighting up the whole altar, the swishing of the cloth the only movement. The ringing faded and the images dimmed and changed.

Jenna was now in the dark, her hands touching what must have been a wooden wall. The surface was rough on her fingertips until they came upon something cool and smooth that felt like metal. It was the dome shape of a bell protruding from the wall. Jenna had the urge to suddenly pull the bell from the wood, except the bell did not come free. Instead, the wall moved forward towards her…

Jenna blinked her eyes and froze, disoriented. She was standing up, breathing hard. The sound bouncing back to her ears indicated she was in a tight area. She had been feeling along the wall with her right hand. Her left hand was high above her head clutching what felt like the stone of her new necklace. She must have taken it from around her neck. The chain was cool against her wrist and forearm. She was holding the gem to the flat surface above her, as if she were trying to make a hole in it with the amethyst. Jenna lowered her arm and it ached briefly as warmness filled it from being up so long.

There was pressure against her back. Where was she? Her hands splayed out in front of her face and met firm resistance of sheetrock. A finished wall, she was sure of it. She could only turn around slowly because of the obstacles by her feet. Now her hands met different kinds of cotton and linen. The telltale sound of a hanger rebounding from losing a garment made Jenna stop. She reached to her side until she found the doorjamb and just outside it, the light switch.

The tube light came to life. A blouse was by her ear and her sneakers were on the floor at her feet. She was in the closet of her bedroom. She stumbled over a heavy sweater and yearbooks on the floor trying to get back out. Once back in her room she peered inside. Nothing had been out of place except her. What had she been doing in there when she should have been in bed?

Once her eyes had adjusted to the light, she looked over at her dresser at the pile on top and finally found what she was looking for. The number she had written was on a corner of a phone book page. She was going to have to transfer that into her address book soon before she lost it. That was something she had never worried about before. She liked to think she was a very methodical and organized person when not otherwise distracted by ghosts and spirits. Her room very seldom had piles of anything, anywhere.

Squinting at the clock, Jenna picked up the phone. Three in the morning or not, this couldn't wait. The phone connected and was picked up before it rang twice. The familiar voice on the other end was neither angry nor surprised by her call. An hour later Jenna hung up, rolled over and fell asleep quickly.

THANKSGIVING HAD STARTED the beginning of the busy holiday season and other than the Full Moon Ceremony, Will and Jenna's personal time on the weekends had been overridden by more pressing activities, for which Jenna was thankful. She wanted more than anything to have her old boyfriend back and have things the way they were, but was scared to be at Will's house without anyone else there. The weekend three days away was a not-family-weekend and would have been the perfect time to have straightened things out. However, Jenna was very involved in the music program at school, especially choir, and her obligations had her everywhere. The school's winter concert was Saturday, the tenth, and the All-County festival was out of town on Sunday.

In between homework and household chores, the evenings of the middle of the week would be saturated too. Christmas caroling at the local Malta house for the senior citizens was scheduled for Tuesday, December thirteenth. That would keep Jenna busy as well, and away from Will who wasn't currently in choir or band. Thursday the fifteenth was the one day both she and Will would work together. It was taken up by a public reading of "A Christmas Carol" by a local author. That was their charity event that supported the local children's hospital. Even the weekend after that was booked—family weekend again. Both Jenna and Will would spend it in school instead on the seventeenth, in preparation for the upcoming exams in January.

Five days after the first package, Monday the twelfth, the second package came in the mail. Jenna had just come home from school, found the box on the table with the rest of the mail, and had immediately taken it into her brother's room.

This one was wrapped the same, in plain brown parcel paper. It was more the size of a necklace box but contained only three loose stones. Each was finished to be worn on a necklace the same way as the amethyst: bound in delicate silver wire with a loop at the top. Jenna felt more at ease receiving this gift as it had a lot more information with it.

Going into her brother's room for anything was a totally odd thing for her to do. She avoided that room as much as possible. It was smelly and dark with clothes scattered on the floor and the curtains drawn to better see his videos on the television screen. Jenna hadn't thought about walking in there, it was an automatic thing she did. The odor was repelling, but something told Jenna she was safer there. The constant feeling of being watched had been bothering her lately, and Peter's after school activities would allow her more than a quiet moment in a place she hoped would keep that uneasy feeling at bay, even if it did smell of sweaty gym socks.

The writing on the enclosed paper was neat but small, and took up the two full sheets of standard size notebook paper. It first started out with a simple greeting and gave an explanation of the stone Jenna wore around her neck. It made sense to learn that amethyst is known to have a direct link to the mind. It also allows the user to rely on intuition as well as clarifying and remembering dreams. It was nice to be validated for wanting to keep the necklace on.

The next paragraph gave a description of the stone Will was wearing with a small definition of its use. She nodded to herself that it was indeed the correct stone. Wondering briefly if she would ever be able to love him the same again, she changed gears and kept reading. The rest of the page explained the meanings of what was inside the box.

The first stone Jenna picked up was a clear quartz crystal. It was rounded, but flat, about the size of a quarter and reminded her of the Herkimer diamonds they had found at the museum. The paper stated that the quartz had healing qualities and acted as a purifier. She was instructed to put the quartz on one side of her amethyst. The next stone was sodalite, dark blue with swirls of lighter blue and a creamy white. It absorbed and neutralized disharmony, negative thoughts, and emotions directed at the wearer by others. She was surprised to learn all the different meanings of stones. Jenna had no idea there were so many for such different things. This, she was to wear on the other side of the amethyst. The last stone in the shallow box was a deep red garnet. She held it up to her eye toward the light fixture, and the room turned crimson. This gem would help provide past-life information and was to be placed next to the quartz.

More information followed. The yellow-looking glass from her dream turned out to be a citrine crystal. This quartz was a cleansing stone, said to dispel sadness and anger. The letter went on to advise that all the stones but one were quartz, a very powerful and prominent crystal, especially in Central New York. The second page surmised the reason for all the psychic and paranormal activity at and around the museum was because the area was rich in quartz. It was said to have the ability to record deep feelings and strong emotional events and were known to replay over and over at times. It went on with more details and gave suggestions and comments.

The last paragraph gave a few choices for the stone she saw briefly in the body of the spider on the scary knife, or the athame. She still had trouble picturing it as that. The one that sounded the most like the stone she saw was a moonstone which was a milky white. That description scared her a little. Moonstone was said to aid in remembering the spiritual events that happen to a person and could assist in seeing the path to someone's desires. It was also a stone that was enhanced by the power of the moon.

"Hmmp," remarked Jenna aloud. She wasn't sure where the phase of the moon was right now, let alone for Yule. She'd have to look into that.

Comfortable with the gift and satisfied with the knowledge she now held, Jenna took off her necklace and reassembled it with the new additions. After putting it back on, Jenna felt a sense of peace and empowerment. She hoped it would give her some real protection as vague as it was, to protect her from something even vaguer.

The extended weather forecast was predicting another nor'easter coming and hitting their area by the end of the next week. She was hoping it wouldn't mess up Yule ceremony. Until then, her mission was to find the crystal she saw in her dream. Unlike the bell, Jenna had a very good feeling where she would find it, if only it wasn't too late already.

That night she settled into bed with purpose, the pendants of her necklace clinking against each other, soothing her. Jenna took a deep breath and exhaled—just as Will and his family taught her—and let each part of her body relax and melt into the soft blankets. She concentrated on the howling of the wind outside her window as she drifted to sleep.

Will's aunts were seated on chairs and sofa around a coffee

table. Half the ladies were drinking wine and the other half, coffee. On the table were several flashlights, an emergency automotive lantern, a small black cauldron, and a little wooden box. The box was open to show a bunch of items for ceremony, only miniature in size.

"I just don't see how it's come to this," Whitty exclaimed, holding her hands to her mouth as her brow furrowed.

"Especially with Sulis, of all people," Lee added.

"She yelled at me the other day when I called," Mina admitted from the adjourning room. "I only suggested we go out for breakfast. She said something about how we've never done that before, and questioned why we would start now."

Whitty's face mirrored the disbelief and shock from everyone in the room. Her eyes filled with tears. "That doesn't make sense. We meet up every few weeks."

"We need to be strong," Diane said, flipping through a thick Book of Shadows. The stones in her rings threw reflections from the flames in the fireplace next to her. "She's not thinking clearly anymore. I know I had a few spells like this in my master book, but never thought I'd need to use them. Ah, here's one."

Mina came over and set a large black duffle bag the table, the sound indicating the weight inside. "I've got more than enough for everyone and lots of fresh batteries."

"Let's go over the words again, it's important to know what we're saying."

The dream morphed and once again Jenna was in the museum, and as expected, a light was illuminating the altar in front of her. She was able to see her likeness as if standing in front of a mirror. It was Sylvia staring back at her with her green eyes. She was wearing clothes similar to what she was wearing the day Jenna and Will fell into the pictures and Sylvia was stabbed by Jonas. Jenna remembered it well. Sylvia was wearing long, dark skirts and a linen blouse with puffy shoulders and tapered sleeves. A tan apron covered them. Her tawny brown hair was again twisted and piled on her head. Jenna's memory seemed to be replaying in the reflection. Sylvia bent down. Jenna could feel herself bend down as well, but still stood, looking into the glass at Sylvia. Sylvia started to place the diamonds in a circle around her, her long skirts swishing. With years of practice they did not disturb the gems. Then a door slamming across the room made Jenna jump. She felt the long, thin citrine crystal in her hand, the bell ringing next to her. The ringing stopped when Jenna's other hand encircled heavy, cold metal, and a piece of parchment paper.

SULIS WAS GETTING frustrated. She had looked over the entire house, at least the parts of the house she could get into. It made her nervous that she needed to admit it was becoming an obsession. She was even dreaming about the thing. Actually, now that she thought about all the odd dreams she had lately, it was always there, somewhere in the background. It wasn't like she didn't have a million crystals of her own. She didn't fully understand why she needed to look for such a particular one. The image of it was etched into her mind. It had five sides, was about three inches long with a notch out of one edge. It was citrine, pale yellow, and a little bigger than the diameter of a penlight. Nothing special or rare; she had seen kinds like these before, except this one *was* special, and she needed to find it. It never crossed her mind to question what she would do with it once she found it. She didn't know now, but would know when she found it. It was a craving that dug into her deeper and deeper.

She was becoming isolated at work because she was so preoccupied and her thoughts were so scattered. She'd even forgotten to do a reading yesterday, something she'd never done before. Her family time was just as disorganized. She hardly spent any time with Will anymore, although he didn't seem upset over it. He was busy these days, too, a lot more engrossed in homework than she'd ever seen him. When a different part of her would nag that she needed to check on her son, she found him on his bed with a book open, reading. If her mind had been working on a cause and effect basis, the days upon days she opened his door would have prompted her to question him. She hadn't realized he had been in the same spot in the same book for over a week.

Her sisters had been calling more. It felt like they were checking up on her and it reminded Sulis of the first few months after Brian died. He had been a healthy young man, in the prime of his life. When she had left that morning to drop the baby off at the sitter's before heading to work, she didn't think twice about him calling in sick, everyone got sick. Shortly after arriving at the office, an uneasy feeling nagged in the back of her mind that something was off. It bothered her all that morning and she tried to call her husband several times to check in on him. When lunch time came she was nearly hysterical and went home. She found him right where he was when she left. Only later did she learn what didn't make any sense at all. Sudden cardiac death. It could have happened to anyone. Her whole world changed from that moment on...

Sulis took in a large breath of air and willed her thoughts to move away from the black memories. There were other more important things on her mind, and her sisters took a backseat to her quest. She had just enough energy for them to set up a date and time for Yule. That should pacify everyone, she thought with a sigh.

As if on a repeating loop, her thoughts went back to the clarity of the crystal. It was five sided, long and slender with a notch out of one end. Pretty pale yellow, cool to the touch...

She began again, moving the camping lantern over another two feet as she searched by hand a new section of the walls in her basement. Her fingers had become so calloused they no longer bled. As her hands explored the courses of jagged rocks, another tiny piece of her mind was pried apart.

In his room, Will was alone. Even Rommy didn't visit him anymore. He sat on his bed with the skull athame and his book next to him, staring at his closet. It wasn't the wardrobe he was seeing; it was blurry, fleeting images of Jenna. His talent to pick up the vibes of others—what he was able to do almost solely with the Ouija board—had been enhanced. The black stone sitting in the hollow of his throat was partly responsible, making his own abilities so much sharper. He had found it in the basement, hanging up by the ceiling of the wooden door. Though he was very learned in stones and gems, he put it on without hesitating. Black onyx was known to hold the memory of physical occurrences surrounding a person as well as cool the ardors of love when worn around the neck. The athame made everything stronger. There was a greater goal in mind and Will didn't think that as much as it would help, it would hinder.

She was close; he could feel it. If only he could see clearly all the time. His vision was often so fuzzy. At other times, when he felt more like himself, he could see everything without difficulty, although this never included Jenna when she was not with him. Will also didn't think to question what he was seeing when his vision was distorted. It didn't dawn on him that it ranged from uncommon to impossible.

"I need to get her to talk, and it's not happening," he said aloud in the empty room. He wrung his scarred hands nervously. Some cuts hadn't healed. Some were fresh.

You need incentive. The light touch is not working. Time is passing too quickly.

The room remained quiet. The voice Will heard distinctly in his ear was a part of him. A defeated look crossed his face. "She knows something isn't right. Her intuition is strong. She's learned to rely on it."

Basic intuition is strong. Human survival instincts are stronger.

Will paused, listening again to what he was told in the silent room and sighed, his face pained. "Yes, I can do that." A wave of sadness passed through him. A part of him was fading away, being pushed aside. Time was running out, and he needed those two things to complete this task. For it is only in the present that a power can be exercised.

Outside the room, Rommy's ears flattened, his fur stood up along his back all the way to the tip of his tail.

Thirteen

HE NEXT FEW days at school seemed both the same as usual and strange at the same time. Even Toby and Tina started to notice a different in Will. It was subtle, nothing more than a change in expression on his face at times. The way he talked seemed different, although they couldn't pinpoint why.

It was Wednesday the fourteenth before Jenna could get together with everyone at the museum. The night before, she had been busy singing for the seniors.

"What was behind the door?" Toby asked, engrossed in her recollection from the dream. He was wearing his favorite shirt, the one with the words, 'If you think this t-shirt looks expensive, you should see my other t-shirt.' Jenna had been unable to talk to him or Tina about it during lunch with Will there. Then Tina's grandmother passed away and she and her family had to leave for Colorado for the services. She wasn't expected back until after Christmas.

The four of them, including Toby's dad and Jenna's, sat inside the tiny museum office. It was getting uncomfortably warm, cramped as they were with all their bulky winter coats, boots, and mixed body heat.

Jenna shifted to her other foot. She wanted to laugh at Toby's choice of attire, but at the moment she just didn't have it in her. "I couldn't tell. But if I'm supposed to be analyzing everything I dream about, we're supposed to all be there for Yule, and I need to bring the bell and that crystal."

"This sounds a lot like Sylvia's doing," Mr. Jacobs admitted.

Jenna nodded. "It must be her."

"Why Sylvia? Why now?" Toby inquired.

"She would be the only one who would have known where the bell was," Jenna answered. "And she practiced white magic. They use bells in their ceremonies. Apparently, she has something to tell us again."

"You also said you feel as if time is running out. Who is trying to get the crystal? Will?" Mr. Jacobs asked, squeaking his hikers in the melted snow.

"I'd say he was. And I doubt Sylvia is sending messages to him. Or Sulis. I'm not sure who is pushing them to find those items."

"Or the skull knife," added Mr. Jacobs. "Who knows what piece of dark magic that stands for."

"I still wish we could get the athame—" Toby began to say.

"Athames," Mr. Stevens corrected.

"I still say if we had the athames we would have the upper hand. At least we have some working knowledge of those. I don't have a clue what the bell and crystal are for," Toby admitted.

Jenna remembered her dreams and knew nothing was specific. "I can't tell you why, but I think they're to unlock a door. At least I have a feeling they are," Jenna offered, although she didn't sound confident either. She kept her eyes down as well, watching Mr. Jacob's boots rub from side to side.

"Are they keys? It could be a metaphoric door, Jenna. For all we know it could open the door to the other world. And if that's the case, then we're all done for because that's what Will and Sulis know best." Mr. Jacobs sighed and the squeaking side to side increased in his frustration.

Jenna had fragments of her dream running about in her head along with what everyone was saying. After she had gotten up the next morning and told her dad about her dream, he had made several phone calls. Too much was going on with school and activities in the evening to think about it in depth, so she found herself here, her head spinning, trying to order her thoughts. It was Mr. Jacobs's boots that finally got through to her.

"Oh, I've just had an epiphany! I've got to go upstairs," she interrupted abruptly, heading toward the door.

"Well, unfortunately, you wouldn't be the first this week," Toby whispered. Everyone looked over at him incredulously.

"Sulis stopped over last night, kinda in a hurry. She muttered something about leaving something upstairs in the loft and said she'd go up alone to get it. Actually, she was kinda rude about it. I knew we had the bell, so I let her. She wasn't up there long, but she did make a racket. She looked pretty put out when she came back down, empty handed, and never even said "hello" or "thanks." Her hair was wilder than it usually is for whatever clients she does readings for on Tuesday evenings, and her eyes were flat and distant. I thought we were safe if she saw for herself that there was nothing there. I didn't think there was any risk…" he trailed off.

"Didn't you follow her?" his father asked.

Toby looked at the floor. "No, I didn't."

His face took on a red hue that Jenna hadn't seen in a very long time. It made her homesick in a way. She opened the office door, and a wave of cool air replaced the stagnant, pent up heat. She walked out and Toby soon caught up.

"It's okay, Toby. You're right. I've been up there before and there wasn't any bell or gem. I just hadn't figured out the crystal thing yet and I think that's where it is."

"Now, come on," Mr. Stevens said skeptically. He and Mr. Jacobs were practically skipping to keep up with Jenna and Toby as they headed upstairs. "We've all seen everything that was on that altar and there wasn't much that was salvageable. We would have definitely seen a large crystal that meets your description."

"We would have," Jenna yelled down behind her, "if it were lying on the altar itself."

Jenna had tossed her jacket on the desk outside the office and made it up the stairs to the second floor. She pulled the ladder over with Toby and headed up into the dark loft first, wondering how on earth Sulis scaled it at all. Right behind her was Toby, puzzled but not hindered. They clicked on the flashlights they had grabbed by the office door almost simultaneously, the beams meeting and intensifying as they passed through Amelie's room to James and Sylvia's.

The altar had been tipped over, although few of its contents had been displaced. The diamond pieces and other stones lay in a loose pile next to it, as if Sulis had gathered them all to inspect and then set them down hard.

"Whoa," Toby exclaimed. "I was so confident she wouldn't find anything I didn't come up here afterwards to see what she did." His face took on a pained look. "I'm not a Pagan but seeing this upended and scattered feels really disrespectful." He picked the altar up gently and righted it. "This makes me nervous, Jenna. Whatever is going on now has Sulis doing things she never would be doing on her own. Who knocks over an altar they pray on?"

The little bit of light that filtered upward illuminated their faces. Jenna tilted her head, a slight smile on her face, as she looked the altar over from several angles with the help from the light. She toyed with her necklace without thinking about it.

By this time Mr. Stevens and Mr. Jacobs had made it up and were stopped short by Toby.

"What is she doing?"

"I don't know, Mr. Stevens." He shook his head. "She has that look on her face. Let's see where this goes. There is no yellow crystal here like she described."

The altar hadn't changed since they discovered it. The shell of a decaying cloth coverlet remained stuck to the wooden stand to house the lumps of candles that time had not destroyed. Jenna set her flashlight next to Toby and picked up the loose stones from the floor, staring at them for a moment. She poured them back and forth from hand to hand. She leaned over the altar and placed the stones back where they belonged. A wicked smile lit up her whole face, and she looked up to Toby.

"Do you still carry your pocket knife?"

Toby hesitated for a fraction of a second, confused, and worried that she might cut herself. Reaching into his pocket, he brought out the knife and opened the blade for Jenna. She took the knife without breaking her gaze with him. She walked around the altar once more before settling on a certain area. Everyone moved in, Mr. Jacobs picking up Jenna's abandoned flashlight. Jenna bent down, her hands caressing the ragged fringe of the coverlet, her eyes distant. She stopped when she grabbed a section and looked up at them peacefully. The blade glinted off the light aimed at her. Toby walked around to her side as an audible rip came from the altar cloth. His light caught up to her hand as she opened it, to display a long, thin, pale yellow crystal.

"It was sewn into the hem of the cloth. It had been Sylvia's skirt at one time," Jenna whispered. She got up and gave the knife back to Toby. She put her hands over the gem, top and bottom, and closed her eyes.

"Yes, this was Sylvia's. She used it for her ceremonies, but she also used this one elsewhere for a different kind of ceremony, one that didn't work out well. What we have in our possessions are the pieces needed to keep something stronger at bay. We need to make sure they go with us to Yule, but no one else can know about them." Jenna's eyes opened, and she looked down into her hands as if seeing the crystal for the first time.

Creaks from below, barely audible had it not been completely silent in the room, alerted them they were not alone. Without thinking about it, Jenna immediately handed the crystal to Toby. He grinned as if being given a dangerous assignment.

"You are the most removed from me, Toby, that's all. Put it in your coat pocket right now," she urged. The sound grew louder and soon footsteps were heard on the loft stairs. Jenna walked away from the altar toward the entrance and came face to face with Will, his flashlight shining on the floorboards.

"Hey, Will. You're just in time to catch up on the renovation ideas for up here," she said calmly. Mr. Stevens was a second behind her, a protective stance to his demeanor. He adopted a more relaxed attitude, following Jenna's lead. Everyone else walked slowly toward them. Mumbling quietly, their muscles tensed.

When the flashlights all caught up, they realized Will looked surprised but not angry at seeing the crowd.

"Well, that is good news indeed, Jenna. I did offer to help with that." They looked at each other for a long moment. More than words were shared in the silence. Will smiled easily and turned back around to the stairs.

"You say we'll make some improvements up there and be able to showcase the altar? There's not much worth seeing, don't you agree?"

"It's a piece of history to this place and the town itself," Jenna replied dryly.

"Yes, so true." Will turned his attention to Mr. Jacobs. "Sorry for the unannounced visit. I haven't been able to find a certain notebook for school and thought I might have left it here the last time I worked. It looks as though it's still missing. Not lost, mind you, just missing. I'm sure it will turn up soon. Sorry for the interruption. Have a pleasant evening." Will's gaze settled on Jenna, his eyes focusing on the necklace that was visible above the scoop neckline of her blouse. A sinister leer washed over his face for an instant before the smile returned as he looked at Jenna.

Without saying more, Will disappeared down the stairs. The front door closing could be heard as they made their way downstairs.

"He had a nasty look for you, Jenna," her father observed. "I don't trust him."

"As convoluted as this sounds, somehow I know that he knows we found the crystal."

"He didn't seem upset by that at all if that's the case," noted Toby suspiciously.

"That's why we have to worry. Whatever his ulterior motives are, it seems like he has a game plan," Mr. Jacobs said, taking off his down vest.

"We're only one week away from taking this head-on. We need a game plan of our own," Toby suggested. They all walked back to the office, wrote notes, brainstormed, and made charts as if they were schematics for a bank heist. With secret plans made for mid-week, they left for the day. The crystal and bell were secured under lock and key.

On the way home, Jenna stared quietly at the dark scenery as her dad drove.

"How exactly do you know Will knows?" he asked.

Jenna was pensive a moment before shrugging her shoulders. "It's like looking at the passing images riding in a car. They just come across my field of thoughts and stick there. I know it sounds weird, but I can tell you I am still my own person. I don't think I can say the same for Will. And now, seeing the altar on its side, Sulis. That's why it's important to stick to our plans. We need to trust each other because when we start doubting that, we've already been defeated."

There was a message waiting for Jenna when she got home. There was a note on the table that her mom was doing last minute Christmas shopping and Peter was at a friend's house, sleeping over. Will had called and wanted a call back.

"Not a good idea. I don't like the thought of you over there by yourself in that huge house. What are they capable of now? I don't know that answer. Until I do, I'm sorry, but you can't go over there alone," he said, in full Dad-mode now.

"Don't worry, I have no desire to. My Will is gone." Jenna stopped right there and thought about the double meaning of that sentence. It was deep. She hoped his will wasn't gone. She missed him.

The rest of the week and weekend went by quicker than Jenna expected. The last few days brought the end of lessons and tests everywhere. Jenna tried to act like nothing was different, but couldn't convince herself. Will seemed to vacillate between the Will she knew and loved, and the strange Will who took to wearing his hair in a ponytail and talking in mannerisms unlike himself.

Sulis never returned the three other phone calls Jenna made to her at home or at work.

The examination preps that Saturday kept her isolated from Will. When she looked at him three rows up from her, he would turn as if called. His smile was not one that made her feel comfortable.

JENNA YAWNED AND stretched under her warm covers. She smiled and was glad it was Sunday, family day. She looked forward to some normalcy. It was the family tradition of getting the tree.

"I can't believe it's already been a year since we've been here last," Peter admitted. They had just arrived at Granger's Tree Farm, the same place they'd been going for the past five years. Jenna hadn't realized just how much her brother had shot up until she saw him against the familiar surroundings.

"Time does go faster the older you get," their dad replied.

"I don't think I'll ever get too old to want to take the tractor to the fields," Jenna said wistfully as she zipped up her ski pants and coat. "Or tromping through the fields to find the perfect tree."

"Even if that perfect tree is always the furthest from the barn and pick-up area, right Jack?"

"Honey, I have no control over the fact that we have to walk a few miles to find the Stevens family tree."

"Yeah," Pete said. "Or the fact that it's usually ten below zero the weekend we go. Good thing I'm growing a moustache." He smoothed down the thin stubble on his upper lip.

Jenna snorted as they stopped at the end of the line for the next wagon and she put her arm around her mother's shoulders. Her mom hugged her back.

"It is cold, isn't it? Let's call it exhilarating. And it's a good thing your father and I spring for hot cocoa and donuts around the wood burning stove in the little lodge. A after you and your father hoist the tree on the car, of course." At this, she elbowed Pete.

"Mmmm. I think that's dad favorite part, actually," Jenna said.

"Donuts are fun. Trying to tie the tree down isn't fun, mom. I get sap everywhere."

"Right of passage, son. You've got it easy, kid. There weren't trails when I was your age. And we had to use twine to pull the tree to the barn instead of these fancy sleds.

"Let's just be thankful we have snow this year," their mom said. "Our first year in Orchard Creek was green and we ended up dragging the tree through mud. We had to stand it up outside by the garage and hose it down."

"Then it froze into a treesicle and we had puddles on the floor everywhere. Up you go," Jenna's father extended a hand to help her up on the wagon steps as the owner, dressed in an oversized Christmas sweater, put his reindeer driving hat on and off they went.

The second half of the day was busy waiting for the branches to thaw enough to decorate while they played really old Christmas music from the seventies and pulled up all the decorations from the basement. Her family laughed and reminisced as they put up the homemade ornaments on the tree that she and her brother had made in elementary school.

It was a special time that meant more to Jenna than the actual presents. It always had.

The top story in the news by that Sunday evening was the weather. Mother Nature was going to deliver the nor'easter a bit earlier than planned. It started snowing Monday evening and continued into Tuesday. It was manageable and school continued without delays. The plowed roadways were kept salted or sanded, depending on the township. By Wednesday, the inclement weather had started to gain the lead, snowing at the rate of about an inch an hour, but school held out until the end of the day. To avoid the nasty weather that was picking up, the district made the decision that Christmas vacation would start on Thursday. Jenna's dad had made arrangements to go with Jenna to the Yule Ceremony which was good because he would have driven her there anyway. It took a lot longer for them to get there, even with a seasoned driver at the wheel. At times he had to search for the road in the pitch-black darkness. There was no reflection shining off the fields of snow for illumination.

Fourteen

*T*HEY FUMBLED UP the walkway to the door, quiet in their own thoughts and worries. Mr. Jacobs and Toby pulled in just as they reached the front steps, so they decided to wait. The wind whipped through their winter coats as if they were wearing spring jackets. They had just enough time to look from face to face before the door opened up with greetings for the night.

The foyer was overflowing with coats, scarves and wet boots. Toby and his dad were wearing matching black jeans. Mr. Jacobs had on a dress shirt under a thin sweater and Toby was for once wearing a long-sleeved button-down shirt. They were welcomed into the green room. They walked in apprehensively, gaping at the beautifully redone interior. Mr. Stevens was close behind, staring the same way as he straightened the collar of his pullover. Jenna smiled, trying to stay relaxed. She wore a pair of cargo pants that looked dressy, along with a three-quarter sleeved blouse that was fitted at her waist and accented her figure. She reached down casually to pat her cargo pocket where she had the bell, then smoothed her shirt and long hair for good measure. Will stayed by her side from the moment she arrived, his rough hand resting lightly on the small of her back.

"You remember my aunts, right?" asked Will. The ladies came over to say hello to everyone, cackling to some inside joke. They were dressed much the same way as they were for the Full Moon Ceremony. Mina was wearing a dress of black velvet. Diane was in a matching dress in burgundy and Lee was wearing a midnight blue button-up blouse and skirt. They all wore make-up and matching silver pentacle necklaces. "This is Mina, Diane, and Lee. Whitty is still in the kitchen."

Toby, Jenna, and their dads shook hands all around. "I think I can keep them all straight now. It's nice to see everyone again," Jenna replied. Instead of handshakes, she got a hug from everyone. Toby rolled his eyes at her after they left. Jenna just shrugged.

"Wonderful! It looks like everyone made it through the storm to join us tonight, thank you. Welcome, merry meet!" Sulis announced, walking into the green room from the red room. Jenna realized she was wearing the same outfit she wore the night they first met. It was a deep cranberry with tiny black beads in the fitted bodice that twinkled like the silver ear clips and necklaces she also wore. A barrette inlaid with three small garnets in her red spiked hair sparkled with every movement she made.

That night seemed like years ago instead of months to Jenna. Her memories of her first encounter made her grin. It was the first time anyone put a name to what she had done with Elizabeth at the museum. What she was able to do. It brought a sense of worry to Jenna that someone as established in their gifts as Sulis could be swayed away from her foundation, something they were going to take on blindly tonight. She suddenly felt very scared and vulnerable.

Whitty popped her head around the corner of the kitchen, wiping her hands on a dish cloth and putting it over her arm waiter style. She was wearing a sheer gold dress. A thin, red fashion scarf was tied around her neck that accessorized with the thin red scarf at her waist.

Sulis picked up a glass of punch and motioned for everyone to do the same. "I'm so excited to have you all here with us tonight. Yule—or the winter solstice—is the longest night of the year. From tomorrow forward we gain daylight as we slowly return to the light. There's an old Celtic story of the dark Holly King, disguised in our world as a wren, being overcome by his brother of sorts, the Oak King of light, who is represented as a robin. The Holly King has had the upper hand, gaining in strength since the summer solstice, when we started to lose light. Tonight, at his strongest, he is overcome by the Oak King. There is always a continuous battle for power. Darkness versus lightness. It's impossible for one to exist without the other."

Everyone held their glass, taking in the meaning of Sulis's last words. Toby looked over at Jenna who glanced at his dad. Will was smiling, watching his mother. There was an overall uncomfortable pause that neither Sulis or Will picked up on. "So, with that, we'll start the night off with some appetizers to nosh on, have ceremony, then see where the night takes us." She raised the glass to her guests and nodded with a smile before drinking. "Enjoy!"

They toasted and sipped their drink. Everyone seemed to fidget with the comment of where the night would go except Sulis and her family. Jenna stepped into the red room to break up the awkwardness. She gave her dad a stern look and he relaxed, making small talk with Diane who was sitting on the sofa. Even though it sounded rehearsed, it very well could have been any family-oriented, mixed gathering.

"Sulis, I'm very impressed with the amount and quality of remodeling you've been able to do here in such a short time span," Mr. Jacobs commented. He was appreciating the delicate trim work around the doorways.

"Thank you. I paint quite a bit, though usually on a much smaller scale. The basics don't change much, so I knew what I was getting myself into. We researched the time period for the house before we closed on it, and I had it all planned out."

"Maybe we should have hired you to help us out at the museum," he confessed, exaggerating as if it was a secret.

"We'll fit in a tour of the house so you can see the rest. The house was remarkable even before the restoration," Will interrupted, stepping away from Jenna. She noticed the onyx necklace under his collar. "Come and see the kitchen. I know you can understand the value of this…"

Mr. Jacobs was led into the kitchen while Will rambled on excitedly about the woodwork and cupboard pulls. Jenna walked over to Toby who had found the food on the large formal dining table and was chewing noisily.

"Wow, Jenna, have you tried this? This is awesome!"

"They're all good cooks, especially Lee and Whitty. Will has told me they make up their very own recipes." Jenna frowned at Toby stuffing his face. He had just put a whole deviled egg in his mouth. One hand held bruschetta and the other was reaching for a stuffed mushroom. "You may want to chew it. You can actually taste flavors better when you don't swallow it whole."

Toby was only able to nod and her annoyance disappeared as their attention was drawn to the instrumental music Sulis had put on the stereo. It was loud, seasonally festive, yet somehow fit with the mystical tone of the evening. Jenna relaxed and looked around the house, trying to see it for the first time the way Toby and their dads did.

"You remember what we have to watch for during ceremony from these two?" he asked quietly in between bites.

"Sure do," Jenna murmured as she wiped peanut butter crumbs from the corner of her mouth, patting her left pocket where the citrine crystal was cradled. She put on a happy face before her stomach twisted in a homesick way as she saw mistletoe hanging from the archway between the green and red rooms. There was silver garland, holly berry leaves and brown twine-like vines framing the pictures and doorways.

"It is a lot to take in all at once," Mina commented, addressing Mr. Stevens as they approached the table.

He put down his punch and nodded. "Your sister is very talented."

"Thank you. She's worked very hard to come this far. She and Will are so happy they settled here. It's a cozy town, too. How long have you lived here?"

Mr. Stevens and Mina engaged in a lengthy conversation about Steel City and the changes he had seen in the few years they had been in Orchard Creek. Jenna got bored of the topic quickly and wandered over to Lee who was sitting in one of the oversized comfy chairs in the tv room. The fireplace was lit and beautifully accented by tiny white lights and green leafy garland. She and Whitty were comparing the ingredients of a dish they both had made and were debating the use of cardamom.

"Merry meet, Jenna! It's so good to see you again!" Whitty hugged her tightly.

Jenna returned the greeting and jumped when Will's hand snuck to her back once more.

"Hey, where've you been?" Jenna asked.

'Hi Aunt Whitty. Taking Mr. Jacobs and Toby on a tour."

Jenna looked around her. "Where are they?"

"Checking out the tapestry. They'll be back in a minute," Will replied with a smile. His eyes were bright with excitement. He brushed his hair back, kissed her briefly on the cheek and went to mingle himself. Mina excused herself and left the room with an armful of papers for ceremony. People came and went from the main rooms and conversations overlapped. The food slowly vanished, and the punch was refreshed. The music rotated on the CD player but never distracted from the atmosphere.

"Jenna, could you get another box of crackers? They're in the far cupboard by the stove," Sulis asked. "They may be hidden in the back somewhere. We'll need them for ceremony."

Jenna nodded obediently, still chewing a piece of celery from the vegetable tray. She went into the vast kitchen, wondering which cupboard by the stove as there were four. She heard the laughter from the entryway behind her and the CD changed, this one playing louder than the last.

"Typical party," Jenna whispered to herself as she started in on the first cupboard. She had gone through three when she turned around, realizing she didn't hear the same droning chatter. She went back without the crackers, stunned that the rooms were empty. Heat crept up her face, and her heart beat louder as she looked around frantically for her dad, Toby, Lee, anyone.

"Hey?" she called meekly. Somehow her air supply was used up.

Will slowly stepped out from behind the archway and stood there motionless, expressionless. "We're starting ceremony, Jenna. You don't want to be late." He didn't move at first, but then held a hand out for her.

Jenna's eyes were drawn to the red on his hands. Seeing the look on her face, he pulled out a handkerchief, spotted with fresh blood, and wiped his fingers. He nodded thoughtfully as he stared at her with that grin on his face. "Why don't you come with me," he began, walking towards her.

"Wha, where is everybody?" she demanded. The force she intended to speak betrayed her. Her hands went to the necklace as if to protect herself, protect it. "Where's Sylvia's athame?"

Will stopped abruptly, his expression faltering before he rearranged it from its momentary slip. "So many questions. All in due time, my dear. We need to get a wiggle on; time is fleeting."

Jenna didn't move. She couldn't move.

"The athame is put away just like I promised."

"Are you using it, Will? Where's my dad? What's with you? Can I see it?" she was definitely goofing this up in a big way but couldn't seem to articulate any of her needs in the right order.

The smile on his face melted all the tension, leaving an angelic and utterly terrifying expression of contentedness. "Ceremony, remember? They're all there."

A whirlwind of thoughts crossed her mind. Never once did she count on being by herself tonight. She had both the crystal and the bell on her person and there was nothing now from stopping Will from taking both. He was much stronger than she, and she was alone. Her feet moved slowly, as if weighted, pulling her closer to the answers, to Will, to her demise. It seemed an eternity before she caught up to him, waiting patiently, his hand extended once more.

"What's happened to you?" Jenna whispered, unable to stop the questions. The comfort she usually found in his eyes was gone, replaced by sardonic curiosity. She could now see the new slices on his hands, the old gashes that were healing and the scars of cuts from weeks ago zigzagging his right hand. Whatever he had been doing, he had been doing it for a while now.

"Hmm. It appears I cut myself." A playful smile teased her.

They walked up the stairs to the unfinished room for ceremony. Ten odd chairs were set around the altar which now had been moved into the center of the room in a circle to accommodate the group.

But there was no group.

Candles that were placed around the corners of the room for lighting illuminated the empty space. Binders sat on six of the chairs. A stack of papers was neatly arranged on the corner of the altar, alone. No one was here. Somehow Jenna hadn't really believed they would be. They had underestimated Will and his mother and their own plans were dead in the water before they even had a chance to implement them.

"How did you cut yourself, Will?" She took a good look at him now even though the only light in the room was candlelight. His eyes still had that wicked gleam to them, his tan shirt was disheveled, wrinkled, spattered with droplets Jenna could only surmise was blood. A corner tear out of one side of his pants was new.

"Now, before we can start ceremony, I need the bell and crystal." He was closing the distance Jenna had put between them. She backed up farther into the room.

"N-no. Where's Toby and my dad?"

"Jenna, don't make me go there."

Jenna just stood there, staring.

"I don't want to dry gulch you, but I will if I have to."

"What??"

"I said I don't want to ambush you for them."

Her voice was shaking audibly now. "I just want to know where everyone is."

"You're kicking up a row and it won't do you any good." His tone was calm but there was anger underneath. Jenna couldn't keep her thoughts straight, and Will was confusing her even more. Now he didn't even make sense when he talked.

"Kicking up a row? Where did that come from? What does that mean? Will, what are you doing?"

Will's voice was pleasant, even, loaded with certainty and confidence. "You're causing a disturbance, ruining this perfect night." He stopped moving. When he began talking again each word was punctuated with meaning. "You know I need them both, and I know you have them."

"You can't have what isn't yours. They never belonged to you," she heard herself say. "Dad?" she called out with futile hope.

"Don't bother, Jenna, you know this house is airtight. It's just you and me now. The weather outside has made all travel impossible, even if you could see your hand in front of your face. A winter storm watch has been put into effect for no roadway traveling until tomorrow afternoon. No school and no work. I've made calls to your house and Toby's for my mother to say everyone would be staying the night until the storm passes. So there's no hurry, but I will win. Give them to me and you won't get hurt."

"Mr. Jacobs and Toby and my dad..." Jenna started defensively.

"They're all dead," Will answered her finally, in a sing-song voice.

Fifteen

IT WAS NOVEMBER 1869 in Orchard Creek. Sylvia was starting to get over the loss of her family. She had covered up the best she could and found reasons for everything that might cause alarm. The gossip from the small town was dying down. At first, after taking care of all the messy details that would create talk, she spent the majority of her days in Amelie's room grieving, crying. When it was time to fix meals for her few remaining boarders she went through the motions. The shock at losing her husband to the fall from the window wasn't hard to show. Telling the ones who questioned where her daughter was cut at her like ice to her chest. Amelie had taken a coach to her family out of town to help with a tragedy there. No one asked about Jonas or Henry, and for that, she was thankful.

The looks the townspeople gave her were not lost on her. It was pity mixed with something else. Hardly anyone looked her in the eyes, but their behavior told her they felt she got what she deserved. She had never attended Sunday sermon with James and any nonconformity bred speculation and rumor. What she did was spend a lot of time in the woods carrying an odd walking stick. The looks on her neighbors' faces said it all. A God-fearing woman wouldn't have been punished by Him this way. A woman who put her faith in God and went to church to pray for straying from the flock wouldn't have lost her husband to such a senseless accident.

She was angry for doubting herself. There had been dreams and visions of losing her daughter but she felt she just worried too much. Now she tried to recall as many visions as she could. There had been so many it frightened her. She hadn't realized the visions gave her the ability to foresee future events.

She had known she would marry a man named James when she started courting briefly at age fourteen. Her visions of being unhappy were filed away, but in hindsight, had been a warning. Major occurrences in her life never surprised her. Looking back, she had accepted things as part of nature or course of life; her mother dying of the sickness, how she would marry in the fall and have difficulty carrying babies, and how her sister would lose her husband to a farming accident. Now she knew, as these occurrences were specific, that she had somehow already expected them. Only now was she able to sum up what that oversight had cost her.

Digging deeper, many of her dreams had involved people in strange clothing with strange tools she hadn't understood. Several visions repeated, getting clearer each time. It was obvious there was the temptation, the lure, to intervene to stop things from happening. Bad things.

However, to acknowledge this ability brought more questions, a new cross to bear. Had she realized and put stock in this gift she had, would she have changed the course of her life? Could she now work with the visions, seeing beyond the present, to change the outcome? She tried to distract herself by staying busy with some minor incantations she had been learning about from her relatives in the New England states, as well as her homeland of Ireland. There were some she was apprehensive about trying. Those balanced that fine line between what she practiced, and something more advanced that called to her.

She wondered if she should try those spells.

After losing four babies she finally had managed to carry and have Amelie. Amelie was her life much more than the man she had married, or rather the man he turned out to be. Precocious and talented, Amelie was her saving grace. The relationship with her daughter was tight and offered her a future. Boarding strangers was never what she wanted to do, but it was what had to be done. James had always been a spontaneous man who had come into money quickly and made poor decisions just as fast.

Fate intervened on a trip into a neighboring town to get supplies before winter settled in. She had just stepped off the porch of the general store when a gunshot rang out close by, spooking the horse tied up front. His loose rein fell free and he reared, nearly stepping on Sylvia. She and her packages fell, and the horse stomped, barely missing her again as he took off.

She stood up, brushed off her skirt, and started to gather her parcels, murmuring to herself, "Thank the Goddess I wasn't hurt."

"Ma'am?" said a tall, thin man bending down to help. His green eyes met hers and an unspoken understanding passed between them.

"Why don't I wind up my business here, and I'll help see you home safely."

Sylvia was surprised to learn the older man with the sandy-colored hair lived in the same town and that they were practically neighbors. His name was Karl, and he had recently moved into town with his young daughter, Elsa. He hardly strayed into his personal affairs other than to say he lost his wife only a few years prior. He was curt about why he left his old home to start anew.

Sylvia had never met anyone who held himself with such confidence, and who, outside her immediate family, was so knowledgeable of witchcraft. He told her he had been practicing for over twenty years and wished to learn of new magic to expand his skills and understanding. Sylvia was a practicing witch with her family—as well as with Amelie—for just as long, and an idea began to thread its way into her thoughts. If she could see what was to happen, couldn't she go backwards and alter the outcome? It was an opportunity to right a wrong that never should have happened.

For weeks, Sylvia and Karl worked together on spells, combining their vast experience. They had quite a few that worked. During that time, Elsa became sick, and Sylvia was feeling more and more uncomfortable with how dark things were becoming. Karl may have been on the side of light when he first started practicing, but it became apparent he tired easily, and desired something stronger and more powerful.

He began doing spells that frightened her, especially after Elsa died. He became selfish and desperate, asking for things in ceremony that were materialistic and unethical. Sylvia worried it would lead bad luck back to them three-fold. Whatever magic was done, good or bad, would come back to the witch threefold, three times more powerful. It was what scared Sylvia. It was what motivated Karl.

Sylvia was glad the relationship they had was platonic and centered only on rites. His temper was as intense as the burning need for gratification in his German eyes, and the pace with which he rubbed his thumb against his finger.

The town folk were talking and drawing assumptions on the goings on at his home with the widow. There had always been an undercurrent of gossip surrounding Sylvia. Now that cloud covered Karl Gruen, the smug immigrant with a fistful of money, who came with only a daughter and no open invitation to anyone.

Sylvia knew the best places for indoor rituals were attics or basements. Even though they always held their practice in his basement, it became a matter of safety as well as privacy. If word got out they were witches, the law would step in as well as the church. And if the sheriff decided to come calling, and proof was found, it would be the end for both of them. Out of necessity, the hidden room was made. One thing Karl was good at was mechanics, and he devised a room so secret, it would require certain items to be used as keys to allow passage inside. It guaranteed only they could get in and only they could use the hidden magic inside the ordinary objects.

IT FELT AS if every ounce of her was peeling away and draining to the floor. Jenna felt the heat leave her face making her cold and numb. She tried to speak, but no sound came out. She stumbled to the nearest chair. She couldn't catch her breath. They were all dead? She thought of the blood on Will's hands. Her breath hitched and stuttered leaving her dizzy, a new ringing in her ears. She knew if she didn't get a hold of herself she would just pass out, and then Will could do whatever he wanted. The pull under was strong. Part of her wanted to go, to get away from the horrible thoughts of what had happened to her family and friends. She tried to fight harder. Will rubbed his hands on the handkerchief once again, oh so slowly moving closer.

He grabbed Jenna roughly by her shoulders. She was groggy, her mind blank, her eyes distant and black. She felt a static rush of energy when Will touched her, and her mind came back awake and raw. She looked up at him unbelieving.

"Dead?"

"Power can only be exercised in the here and now. My pain is unbearable and it is mocked by those who no longer feel that pain. Do you know what it's like to lose your family? To see others who have moved on when you cannot? They must be made to suffer as I have."

Jenna processed that. His family was here. Who was he talking about? A sudden intake of breath passed her lips as she realized this wasn't Will talking. Several things started to make sense; she needed to get out of this room, get away from Will, and the odds were stacked against her. She leaned forward as if falling, and Will let go of her. She got up gradually and stumbled into the empty space of the room between the chairs and door, holding her head, her eyes closed. Will stood still except for his thumb stroking his finger and his tongue passing over his lips, a hungry anticipation to his demeanor. He eyed her movements; anxious, waiting. She groaned, her hand fumbling on the wall for balance. She drew in a large breath and bolted from the room, tearing around the corner and praying her body didn't overtake her feet on the stairs.

A snarl of frustration followed closely behind her. She pounded down the stairs, just getting to the fifth one before she heard Will hit them himself. She slipped on the bare floor on the landing before catching her balance and ran flat out through the green room on legs she could no longer feel, desperately searching for a way to stay away from him to escape. Her long hair, flowing behind her, was snagged just as she reached the archway. She screamed as her head jerked upward, her feet pulled back with force. The music continued loudly, a madrigal round spiraling in on itself, contrasting to the aggression in the room.

Abruptly she was wheeled around, face to face, with Will. His grasp was lighter, his eyes tortured and hurting as an internal battle was brewing inside him. "Please, don't make me do this! I love you, Jenna."

For half the time it took to blink, Jenna was conflicted. She was surprised to find herself kissing Will, full and deep under the mistletoe. This was her Will, and he was here if only for the briefest of seconds.

"Don't do it. Don't lose your will. Stay with me, I love you, too." As soon as the words left her lips, she took off again, this time towards the stairs in the kitchen that led to the basement, a strategy formulating.

Will hesitated but was upon her by the time she reached them, an unnerving growling sound growing as he caught up, quicker than she anticipated. There was only one choice to protect herself and she hated to do it. She threw her body onto the sturdy door to the basement, one hand grabbing the bare coat hook with her weight and the other clasping the door knob. She held on for dear life, her head turned in Will's direction, turning the handle and bracing for impact. As Will lunged to seize her, the door swung away making him miss completely. He continued forward, falling down the stairs. Jenna's brain processed it in slow motion: the pain, anger, and betrayal crossing his face as his hands shot out, clawing at nothing but air as he disappeared down the stairs.

It was quiet. That didn't make a difference in this house. Will had told her that the first time she visited. The house was tight. Silence and noise were irrelevant now, anyway. The moonless storm outside whipped everything into an everlasting whiteout that closed all the roadways from travel for the night, isolating the house from the world. And now time had stopped.

The door swung back, rebounding. Jenna clambered off as soon as she could reach the kitchen floor, and flicked on the light switch. She turned back and forth, wanting to go downstairs to see if Will was okay but knowing she needed better light to do it. She did not want to leave her position in case he came back for her. She squinted into the darkness of the basement, seeing no movement.

She turned again into the kitchen, feverishly throwing open drawers, unable to remember which one Will had gotten the flashlight from during her first visit. The fourth drawer she pulled had a lot of miscellaneous items like staplers, pens, screwdrivers and flashlights. The flashlights all looked alike. Choosing one, she hoped the light she grabbed was not the one that needed batteries.

Shaking, she started down the hard, steep stairs, realization creeping into her that she might have inadvertently killed Will herself. He was there, a short distance from the last step, face down, arms splayed. She shined the flashlight on him for several seconds, looking for the rise and fall of his breathing. The beam of light trembled with Jenna's nerves. He was breathing shallowly and Jenna dared not touch him. She didn't know what damage she had caused, but also didn't know if he would come to in the next few minutes and attack again.

The longer she was in the basement, the more she thought she heard muffled voices. Light bounced from every corner as her flashlight looked for more obstacles. Her mind couldn't wrap around the fact that Will was beat up, covered in blood, and channeling something akin to a demon. Why else would he kill his own family and attempt to hurt her, too? Hollowness lay on her like a thick quilt, making these thoughts hard to process. Self-preservation took in every detail, every breath, and every movement she made. It was categorized and filed if not immediately necessary for her survival.

Jenna found herself drawn to the canning cellar in the far-right corner of the basement. Somehow, she knew she would end up there. It was the only place that made sense now. She passed the cistern on her right as she held her necklace in her hand tightly, hoping the key would still be there on the peg next to the canning cellar. The light traced the wall but found nothing. The pinching feeling in her stomach got worse.

"No, no, no, please, let it be here," pleaded Jenna, her

right hand rubbing the stones of her necklace frantically. She stopped and made herself take a deep breath. She tried to clear her mind and found it easy to do. Maybe it was the dull numbness that blanketed her, protecting her, like losing one sense and gaining a sharper one in return. Maybe her focus was just that much more intense because her life depended on it, like the hunch she had a few weeks back and called Will's aunt. She thought about necklace and all the stones that Mina had sent her and the magic they held. Jenna was powerful with the natural abilities she had been given, and the stones made that stronger. She took a deep breath again. Images crossed her mind's eye and passed. The cistern passed twice, and Jenna knew she had her answer.

She backtracked towards Will, keeping her distance, the flashlight holding out after all. He was still in the same position she had found him in, still breathing evenly. She left him and walked the few steps to the cistern, which was like a deep hot tub without water, and looked inside. Off in one corner the light shown on the rusty skeleton key. With some effort, she started climbing to retrieve it and slid into the basin instead.

Not even a minute had passed since she came down to the basement, but in a way, it felt like forever, and she worried about how much time had gone by. Time was running out, she could feel it. How long would it be before the man showed up here? He followed her, she knew that. He had manifested. He was a part of Will somehow, she knew that, too.

Jenna huffed as she climbed back out of the empty tank and was still shaking when she reached the canning cellar door. Jenna pushed the key in and reached down to make sure the bell was still in the pocket of her cargo pants. Somehow she knew she needed to have them. The pocket was empty of something that large. She felt the citrine crystal wand at the bottom, but nothing else. Panic gripped her as the voices grew louder. She didn't understand the voices but it made no difference and barely registered in her mind. Her attention focused on finding the bell. Will could not be allowed to get it. It could have fallen out anywhere. She tried to replay the last hour and was disturbed to find she could not. "Take a deep breath, breathe. Concentrate," she said to herself aloud. Her wrinkled forehead smoothed. The fine hairs that usually tickled her face did not. The cistern again crossed through her mind. With borrowed calmness she quickly walked back to the cistern and flashed the light inside. The bell was there, plain as day. It must have fallen out of her pocket when she ungracefully fell into it to retrieve the key. With her energy stores depleting quickly, it took longer to climb in, get it, and get out. The only sound in the room was the Velcro clasp opening and closing on her cargos as she slipped the bell inside. Half jogging to the canning cellar door, she jumped as shadows emerged from the darkness.

She had let her guard down for a moment and should have taken inventory again of her surroundings. Thoughts of being too late ricocheted and echoed around her brain. Her scream was loud enough that it could have been heard throughout the entire house. The agitated voices grew clearer.

Sixteen

INA AND WHITTY ran out from the center of the basement from the concealment of the storage totes. Jenna was being embraced, calmed by soothing voices, her hair smoothed before she realized she was still safe. For an awful moment she thought the shadows were of the man and would attack her alone and unguarded. Her eyes were bugging out, looking through the people who held her, her mind unable to comprehend the friendly faces. One of the ladies turned the key that Jenna had fit into the lock of the canning cellar door. The metal scraped against itself as the key was retrieved. The door opened to a pitch-black void. The tiny cellar window was completely covered by the snow outside.

"Oh, that's right. Sulis hasn't had electricity run in here yet," Mina remembered. Several flashlights and one lantern lit up the dark, empty room. They were prepared.

"Are you all right? Are you hurt?" Mina asked, looking

Jenna over carefully. Mina frowned and picked up Jenna's wrist to feel her pulse. The glazed expression on Jenna's face worried her. She didn't show any emotion. She did not seem relieved or happy to see them at all.

"They're all dead. Dead," repeated Jenna flatly.

"If I didn't know any better, I'd think she's in shock, Whit. I don't know if we can work with her like this."

"She's going to have to be. Will's been out for about three minutes. We can't guarantee that he won't wake up. If we get locked in that room, no one will ever find us," Whitty warned, escorting Jenna through the doorway, closing the door behind them. More voices in here, almost distinctive.

"Hold on, we're coming!" Mina called to the empty room.

Jenna didn't understand what was happening and why two of Will's aunts were still alive. Were they talking to spirits? For an instant Jenna wondered if they were ghosts like Jonas and Seth. Mina's face suddenly appeared in front of hers, a strong light shining up towards the ceiling, giving light to everything at once.

"Jenna, the men are here, and we need your help. Remember what we talked about on the phone? Remember your dreams? You have the keys to unlock this door, and only you can do that. Honey, we have to hurry," she urged gently.

Jenna started to blink, her eyes dry. She looked around at the women, and it caught up to her. She did have a mission here. She remembered. She reached into her pants pocket and took out the bell. She reached in again and pulled out the crystal. Yes, she knew she needed these things.

Nudged again, Jenna started to walk towards the tiny nook, but hesitated.

"Jenna, think about your dream. We believe Sylvia has been helping you. Let your thoughts and memories guide you. All our energy is directed at you," encouraged Mina.

"No, Sulis," Jenna began, confused, shaking her head back and forth.

"Right now, it's you. Sulis is upstairs with our sisters. We believe Sylvia might have been trying to contact Sulis as well, but Sulis has been, in a way, desensitized. The little we got out of Will through our phone calls to him is the name Karl Gruen. He told us he was the former owner. When you told me about the skull athame and then the necklace Will is now wearing, we tried to put the pieces together. We thought we had figured it out, at least that there were things that Will and Sissy were looking for. But Sulis hasn't sounded like herself, she's been so distracted. And from what you've told me about Will, there was little doubt. Anyway, when we stepped inside the house tonight, we could feel it ourselves. This place is saturated with what must be Karl. That presence is stronger here." Jenna looked at Mina blankly and Mina paused before trying again. "It's like being in a home with strong cinnamon in it. After a while you can't smell it, even though it's still there. Will, and Sulis, have become immune to Sylvia because this place is so thick with dark magic." Whitty nodded somberly in agreement.

It sounded right. Will had definitely been distracted lately and Sulis wasn't herself either. Jenna alone went the few steps into the tiny alcove to the end, followed by Whitty, while Mina stayed behind and shown her flashlight towards them. Whitty's flashlight lit up the area in front of Jenna. The wooden board was illuminated. There were so many holes and so many areas with new dig marks. Which one was for the bell? Did it matter? Her hands started to tremble. Suddenly, Whitty's warm hands were on her shoulders comforting her. "You were drawn to the bell and citrine for something specific. What you told me Mr. Jacobs suggested sounds right. Those things must be keys. Concentrate and allow yourself to be led."

Jenna closed her eyes and took a deep breath. She skimmed the past and found herself at the night she woke up in her closet. It had seemed like she was climbing her wall, searching for the place her amethyst fit into. Particularly the topmost part of the left corner. Was that the action she needed to do? Holding the citrine in her left hand, she reached up high and forced herself to relax. Without the aid of her vision, she found a small hole way up and to the left from the center of a knot. The crystal fit snuggly. She opened her eyes.

In her right hand, she held the bell by the curve and looked around for what felt right. She was aware of several different voices directly in front of her, sounding very much like her dad, Toby, and Mr. Jacobs. The flashlight mirrored Jenna's gaze and she found a thin notch with a wider center. The crown of the bell fit perfectly. She pushed them both until they hit resistance. Without thinking, she found herself twisting the bell clockwise, a ping sound coming from somewhere inside. Looking over her shoulder, Whitty smiled at her. "Now what?"

Jenna pulled and the large slab moved toward her, a doorway into a concealed room, occupied in the darkness by her father and friends, alive and well. Jenna was embraced by her father, holding her and telling her over and over how happy he was to see her. Toby and Mr. Jacobs slapped Mr. Stevens on the back, relief evident on their shadowed faces.

"Hey, can I get a light in here?" Mr. Jacobs asked. A flashlight was passed over and he disappeared back into the room, a faint light emanating from the small cubby. "There's an altar in here," Mr. Jacobs reported.

"Are you sure that's what it is?" Mr. Stevens questioned. "Not a table? It still looks like a sliced off piece of tree trunk to me."

"That's two feet tall, two feet wide, and smooth on the top? Sitting in the middle of a hidden room? It reminds me of Sylvia's. I'd say it was an altar," Mr. Jacobs rebutted.

"The most conducive rooms to practice in are the ones highest and lowest," Mina said from the around the corner. "Remember, when Sylvia was practicing it was the 1800's and the idea of witchcraft wasn't thought of fondly."

Jenna turned the bell back to its original position to pull the door open wider for everyone to leave when the door pinged once more, and something small fell on her foot. Jenna let out a little squeak, startled. Everyone looked down to see what appeared to be a piece of wood or the knot from a piece of wood.

Mina called to them from the middle of the room. She was too large to fit in the alcove. "What it is? What's going on?"

"It looks like it might be an amulet of some sort! This must be what Will was searching for and why he needed the crystal and bell," Whitty exclaimed, holding the flashlight as close as she could. "It's obvious he didn't need the bell and crystal to get the door open."

"Although he certainly wanted them bad enough," Mr. Jacobs added, frowning with the thought. He leaned over to see, the light illuminating a red scratch down his face.

"He used that skull athame to pry open the door," Toby stated as he bent down and picked up the object.

"What is it?" Mina asked again.

"It looks like a piece of wood or a river stone. It's not very heavy," Toby stated, the amulet bobbing it in his hand as he gauged it's weight. He turned it over, scrutinizing it closely. It was brown on one side and the color nearly made it camouflaged while in the side of the door. It looked more like a stone except that it was black on one half and white on the other. "Huh. It doesn't seem like it was painted or stained. These colors are natural." He handed the amulet to Jenna who took it without commenting.

"That was pushed out by the bell?" asked Mr. Stevens, looking over the door with the crowd. "Oh, I get it. You can see the tension the bell put on this part here once it was inserted. As it was turned, it allowed the wood piece to drop into position to be pushed out when the bell was turned back." He shifted his face towards the cubby entrance. "Sort of like gum in a gumball machine," he explained, loud enough for Mina to hear from the main room.

"Well, this keeps getting more interesting," Mr. Jacobs voice carried to them. He appeared in the doorway, a dry rustling sound getting louder with the strength of the light as he neared them. "It was dark in here, but it didn't stop us from trying to get out. We kept bumping into this stump in the middle of the room. We also searched the walls by hand. One stone felt loose. I just pulled this out."

The flashlights centered on a browned piece of parchment paper. It was passed through to Whitty. Everyone leaned in to see.

"This is amazing. It's a spell," Whitty said. She began to leave the alcove back to the center of the room, her flashlight concentrated on the center of the parchment as she read the faint words. "This is going to blow your minds. I think it's Sylvia's and it sounds like this will end what's going on here."

"Hold on. What does Sylvia have to do with that or this house if it was that guy Karl's?" Toby asked. "Everything we've found out about him leads us to the kind of witchcraft Sylvia wouldn't do."

"Not everyone practices white magic, Toby," Mina stated.

"Right," answered Toby. "So, this doesn't make sense."

"I guess we'll never know," Mr. Stevens said, resigned.

"Actually, we do know," Witty interjected, studying the brittle paper. Everyone followed Whitty out. Jenna, who had been watching like a bystander, was pushed by the crowd. The men hovered into a circle around the two women. Jenna stood there awkwardly, still holding the round amulet, looking at each of the men's faces with a worried expression.

"What's wrong with Jenna?" Toby asked. "She's acting funny."

"I'm not sure, but she seemed to be under the assumption we were all dead. I think that threw her for a loop," Mina replied quietly.

"I'm okay, I'm okay," Jenna said, trying to accept the reality she was seeing. She gave the amulet to Mina and, wiping her face with her sleeve, leaned in as her dad hugged her again. Toby and Mr. Jacobs hugged her briefly as well.

"It really is a spell? In a canning cellar? How do you know?" Toby asked.

"I know a spell when I see one."

"I'm sure this was the room they used to practice. But sister, don't you think, if it was, they would have had plenty of spells in here?" doubted Mina. She turned the round object over as she studied it.

"Of course they would. But this paper says so right here. At first, Sylvia and Karl found companionship in grieving their spouses, although he still held a lot of anger. It seemed he was trying to find peace so she joined him and they began working with trigger objects. But then his only child died. He became consumed with lashing out and punishing others. His focus went deeper. The darker the witchcraft he experimented with, the more his power increased to connect with his essence regardless of living state. At that point, she believed he targeted anyone who had gotten over the death of a loved one. When Sylvia realized this was his only intention, she tried to distance herself from him but couldn't. His talismans had been charged with intention. If he wasn't able to achieve his goal in his lifetime, he would be able to after death. If they were touched or moved, it could pave the way for him to try to cross over to continue his quest."

No one spoke for a moment as they absorbed what that meant.

"Sylvia did achieve something like that—crossing over I

mean—with the turquoise candle," Mr. Jacobs stated. "And the pictures of the museum with the date on them. She had trigger objects, too."

"But none of them achieved their ultimate goal on their own. They were flawed. Sulis and Jenna had to help," Mr. Stevens admitted, frowning.

"Magic is not always predictable," Mina added. "And that's a lot of power to call on and rein in."

"That's why Will wanted to know what I was thinking and dreaming about," Jenna gasped. "I have a connection to Sylvia."

"Yes. And Sylvia was definitely connected to Sulis," Toby said.

Jenna took the delicate paper that Whitty held out, skimming it. She read on. "I have come to regret how far I've gone with conjuring and will need help from my future sisters of the craft who have visions like myself. I have crossed beyond the white magic of my core with Karl to hidden corners of power that should not have been disturbed. I have helped awaken the consort of darkness, and cannot stop Karl on my own. It has been set into motion and cannot fully be taken back. All I can offer now is the intention I've secretly set in the amulet. He believes it's been charged for his spell work. Alone, my magic is weak but together with the strength of my athame and the influence of others whose gifts are earth-based, I believe the black magic can be unraveled and removed for good."

The parchment was passed around, crinkling in the silence.

"How could she have known…?" Mr. Stevens asked.

"Sylvia has known just about everything. She has guided us many times as long as there was an opening. We need to do this," Jenna murmured, taking the amulet Mina held out to her.

"We were going to do a banishing ritual and possibly one for possession here tonight to intervene with this negative energy, but it will be more effective coupled with this. We've lost precious time. We need to hurry," Mina told them. She turned and started to pull things out of a medium-sized satchel slung over her body.

"How did you get here?" Jenna asked her father.

"Forced by Will," her dad answered at the same time Mr. Jacobs talked.

"You know, we're going to have a few choice words for Will when this gets straightened out," he continued, rubbing the mark on his face.

"That's not Will, Mr. Jacobs. Something else is making him do this," Jenna interrupted.

"We figured as much after that fact."

"I can't believe I walked down here and was tricked into being locked up," admitted Mr. Stevens with a scowl. The side of his shirt had a small rip in it.

"Some tour of the house. Dad wasn't around and it never dawned on me to worry about that," Toby said. "Then I actually walked into this room on my own. He had a candle lit and everything. Of course, by the time I started into the alcove here, he had taken out that athame."

"We tried to get out when Will brought down your dad, but we couldn't get around him. That athame is too sharp," Mr. Jacobs said.

"Yeah, and somehow Will is very strong," admitted Toby, quietly.

"We'll need to catch up on the details later, time is flying. Lee should be here shortly with the others and we can do this right here." Mina turned to Whitty. "Do you have everything you need?"

"I have everything but the two athames," answered Whitty as she headed for the canning cellar door. "If you gentlemen would accompany me, I need to see if Will is still carrying one."

"Oh, he was. That is one mean athame. It's worse when you're looking at the business end of it. I'll go out with you," Toby offered, stepping around Jenna's dad. A cut above his ear and across his back of his hand were the only signs of his struggle with Will.

The door creaked open and Whitty popped her head out the room's door and flashed the light towards Will.

"Oh dear, we're in trouble! Will's gone."

Seventeen

ℰVERYONE GATHERED TO look except Mina who hesitantly stepped out into the cellar and asked for Toby to follow her. In a moment they were back, each carrying an end of one of the plastic totes that held old curtains and bedding linens. She motioned for it to be set down by the far wall and brought out items from the satchel.

"This is a travel altar kit and this tote is going to hold our makeshift altar," Mina advised, taking out tea light candles, stones, a salt cellar, a bell, lighter, and incense cone. At the bottom was a wooden plaque that had a pentacle burned into it. She reached in the bag again and brought out a small cauldron. By her foot was a large black duffle that Jenna must have overlooked. Mina pulled the drawstrings apart, revealing a bunch of small black boxes and passed them around, turning the knob on the one she kept. The small room was immediately filled with loud static.

"You brought walkie-talkies?" Toby asked, astonished.

"This is in our skill set; we've done a lot of interventions over the years. What we learned from the calls Jenna made, Will and maybe Sulis were somehow incapacitated or impaired. Sulis is very powerful and her mind is not easily swayed, and Will is very much like his mother. Whatever was here was strong and would need intervening. And if something was going on like that with both of them, they might be split up, which would mean we would be split up. This house is huge. Of course we had no idea what exactly *was* happening here, so we made many general plans. From what Jenna told us, it sounded like possession, so that's what we brushed up on. That's very serious and we're not taking that lightly."

"Oh," was all Toby said. He looked at Mina who was calling her sister.

"Lee, come in."

"What's the word, Mina?"

"We need to do this now. Will is somewhere in the house and has the athame on him. He had managed to lock everyone up in the cubby in the basement."

Whitty bent down and a click sounded. Mina's voice echoed as Witty attached the unit to somewhere on the belt of her dress that matched her festive scarf.

"Sissy heard that. Do you have all the items?" asked the voice on the other end. Toby looked at Jenna, confused. Jenna mouthed Sulis's name and he nodded.

"No, but we've realized we need Karl's and Sylvia's athames. Will has to get the piece out after all and this is the place. Do you need our help?"

"Negatory on that. Sylvia's athame is secured with us."

"Okay, five minutes. Be safe." Mina signed off. "We've gotta move, let's roll," she announced. Mr. Jacobs and Toby were confused.

"We're smarter than the average bear, Mr. Jacobs," Whitty said. "We took precautions and rehearsed some common words and phrases to stay elusive. "Be safe" has hopefully alerted Diane and Lee to the fact that we aren't, at this particular moment, in control. Lee and Diane have Sulis upstairs. We also told them we need to do the ceremony here."

"I thought we had the other piece," Jenna admitted, turning the amulet over in her hand.

"We do, honey, but Will doesn't know that. He might be right outside their room for all we know. We want him to come here of his own volition. We don't want anyone hurt." Mina held her hand out, and Jenna handed the amulet and parchment over without question. Mina set them on the make-shift altar.

Jenna's father came back in from keeping a watch at the door. "If we need to do the spell here, why are we leaving?"

"When Lee said "negatory," she was telling us she needs help. If they're able to, they'll make their way down. But if Will intersects Sulis, they will need a hand. And rooms that have been used for practice hold the most energy. So yes, we need to do this one here," Whitty answered.

"We figured when Will started disappearing with your friends and returning alone, we needed to watch him," Mina stated. "We wanted them separated until we knew what we were doing so Lee lured Sulis upstairs with a question for the seating. She and Diane managed to hide her. We've had some radio contact with them that confirms she is under some sort of influence."

"I don't like the idea of splitting up again. We were caught totally off guard earlier. His game plan was simple, but effective, and it wasn't even dealing with these trinkets or the ceremony. He's going to have this place covered like Fort Knox so he can complete whatever business this Karl guy has to do," Mr. Stevens stated frowning.

"We do have communication, and there are three males here," offered Mina. She had not stopped setting up and organizing the altar. There was a moment of hesitation.

Mr. Stevens exhaled, resigned. "Who stays and who goes? Who needs the most help?"

"One should stay, two should go," Whitty and Mina said together.

WILL OPENED HIS eyes, disoriented, hurting. For a fleeting moment, his thoughts remained quiet. Why was he on the floor of the basement? Was it day or night?

You have been chiseled by the girl. She has what we need. It might not be too late.

In a moment of clarity, the fog around his brain cleared and he realized everything he had been doing, working towards, was not from his own mind. His free will had been replaced with a monster's quest. How could he not have seen it before? Karl had ordered him to kill to get those odd pieces so that his own deeds could be completed.

Will realized he had only vague memories of the past few weeks. It felt like watching everything through a white screen. He was a part of it although it didn't feel like him. Will remembered how rough he had been with Jenna.

"I don't want to do this anymore," Will whimpered.

Hobble your lip! You should have done what I told you to when you had the chance.

Will got up slowly, his feet fumbling to plant themselves firmly on the level ground. He touched the right side of his head; a small part felt sticky. A wave of vertigo washed over him from the blood rush, and his body ached practically everywhere. Quietly he took the steps to the main level of the house.

Music was playing, but the room was empty. All his plans for this evening were wrong. Jenna! His mind searched for any memories of harming her. He remembered running after her, his grip on the athame in his waistband, waiting to take what he needed if she refused. Emotions swirled with the thoughts that lingered on her kissing him, and he raised his hand, his fingers touching where her lips met his. He remembered feeling the fissure in his own mind, breaking away from the cloud that metastasized into his very being. He stopped at the sink to rinse the blood from his elbow and head. "No," he said firmly to himself. "I'm not going to do this anymore."

The challenge was taken up. Suddenly Will was unable to breathe, the pressure in his ribs compounding the pain in his head.

It's time to hunt, boy. I can smell her.

Will gripped the porcelain, his mind racing. Suddenly, air

rushed back into his chest, allowing him to gulp it noisily. The dizziness subsided. He looked down at his hands, red and sore.

You will do what I tell you to do. If we get the citrine and bell, your hands won't hurt by using the athame to jemmy the door.

Will's thoughts went back to Jenna. There must be a way to save her.

Stop thinking about her! She's only necessary for the tallismans. Once I have those, I can continue with what I set out to do. What needs to be done. So many need to be punished.

Will shook his head in bewilderment.

The death of family leaves a mark I learned to detect. And those who broke their pledge, who found happiness again never truly loved, I tell you. They soiled the sacredness of vows, and they aren't worth the air they're tasting. They deserve to suffer, the whole lot of them. I was faithful. I mourned to keep her name alive, and what did I get for that devotion? The loss of my daughter as well. Whatever god there is deserves to watch the professed faithful fall. And an eye for an eye is not an even payment.

Will tried not to think of what he needed to do. Of course everything this voice told him centered on getting even with those who were unlike him. Will knew his thoughts. Karl's wife had died during childbirth. The only woman he had ever loved, only ten short months, lost while giving him the child he always wanted. The need for acceptance he had never found in his childhood carried over, and the one time he had let his guard down, he lost it all. There was no trust in anything from that moment on. He became incensed at anyone who had pulled themselves up by their bootstraps and continued on. He would use who he needed to get what he wanted, and that was all. This older girl, Jenna, stood in his way just as Sylvia had.

When Will tried to think of Jenna, awful ideas surfaced. The thoughts produced from Karl stung and festered like a hornet's nest. It made Will wince to have those images in his head. It made him angry, a kind of angry he wanted to act on.

Then get up and be a man! She can't be allowed to best you.

This was dangerous. Will was bound to do this business. Now he realized he needed his mother and aunts more than ever. He had been infuriated when he first saw the protective necklace Jenna had on. The fury wasn't his own, he was realizing now. The stones could only have come from someone who knew gemology, and Will was sure Jenna's only connection was his family. A connection he had been drifting away from for the last month due to this drive.

Will frowned when he thought about the continuous obsession that pushed him to do things he never would have done on his own. His mother had been doing that as well. Will knew she had a need to search the house for the missing pieces. That was her job. All the while, he went about his regular life at school, somehow able to concentrate on his studies. How could he not see what he was enveloped in at home? His mind was trapped in a scrim of another's bidding. He never gave it a thought on why his mother hadn't kept up with the housework, or made dinner, or did anything else except search their home. The house had turned up nothing. Will remembered how they were becoming desperate, and how his mother took a risk and climbed the ladder at the museum to check over the altar.

A malevolent smile played at the corners of Will's mouth

without his permission. He knew when Jenna had the bell and tiny citrine wand. He felt it. He had seen both in her hands through the haze his thoughts brought him when he sat in his room. Karl's old room. The drive to find Jenna and take what she was hiding was strong. And it also made him mad. She lied! The fury he felt towards her was scary. Even worse, he didn't trust what he would do when he caught her. Like forcing a partition closed in his mind, Will tried to push Karl's urges to the side but they were too strong.

"Stop it!"

You best be satisfied I've let your mind wander. Fear only gives me more power, boy. Women should be submissive, and know their place is not at the head of the table. None of them can be trusted. Sylvia defied me, taking the bell and hiding the citrine, knowing full well the amulet would remain locked away without them. No matter. Soon I will have everything I need, and all will be well.

Will felt hopeless that everything rested on whether anyone had figured out what was really going on and how they planned to fix it. Without his beckoning, his legs carried him to retrieve Sylvia's athame he knew was in his mother's possession.

"I'M STAYING," JACK declared, his large hands squeezing Jenna's shoulders.

"Cool. I'd love a little revenge with the boy toy."

"That's not fair, Toby. Will is under the influence of something stronger than himself. I'd like to think he would have beaten this intrusive entity if he weren't living inside it, and subsequently it inside him," Mina scolded.

"I know, I know, I'm just sore I got locked down here without a hint of what he was up to. It's bruised my ego, among other things," Toby admitted, rubbing his bicep.

"You're a big man, Toby. Glad you can own up to that. Remember, he has the advantage of knowing this house very, very well. We want everyone down here safely so we can have this blessed ceremony and put things right."

"Sure," Mr. Jacobs said sarcastically.

"It could be that simple, but don't underestimate the gravity of this. The last time we talked with Diane and Lee it sounded like they had gotten through to Sulis but after some intervention. Those athames on the loose are very dangerous. Energy is stored in the tools we use for spell work. What type of energy is stored in those athames is unknown. None of us know what they are capable of doing together. If everyday objects have been turned into talisman, the potential for this to get ugly is very high," Whitty piped up.

Mr. Stevens and Mr. Jacobs looked at each other nervously. They knew the potential for ugly from only a few months before. It had been a close call that they hadn't lost one of their own.

"Okay ladies, what's your plan now?" asked Mr. Stevens. He had not left Jenna's side.

"We need Karl's athame and Sissy. She is in one of the rooms upstairs now. Unfortunately, it's on the other side of the house from here. We need someone to go up and make sure all three of them get down here safely."

"What about Will," Jenna asked. Her mind, although muddled, was starting to reconcile what didn't add up. What Will had told her was nothing more than a vicious lie. Even though she could see, touch, and talk to her father and friends, part of her didn't want to get too comfortable. Her reality had been damaged.

"We're open to suggestions."

Toby took an extra walkie-talkie from Mina, tuned in on her channel, and stuffed it into the waist of his jeans. A feeling of déjà vu from Halloween seemed to order Jenna's thoughts. It pushed away the black hole of emptiness she felt without Will next to her.

"He still wants me. I'm the one who knows the secrets. He needs to find me," Jenna offered, knowing she was right the more she talked.

"Absolutely not!" her father nearly shouted before she got the last words out of her mouth.

"If it's not Will who wants me, it's Karl. I know he is not happy I tricked him. Besides, I know the house—"

"Jenna, that is not going to happen." Mr. Stevens was whipping his head as if trying to shake out the possibility of this suggestion.

"Jack, maybe you should stand down. We need him. She has a good point," suggested Mr. Jacobs quietly. Mr. Stevens did stop. He was speechless. His mouth gaped open at his friend.

"Gentlemen, the time," reminded Mina gently.

"I can't, this has come so close, and it's not the only time…" Mr. Stevens fizzled out, his frustration and fear mixing with anger.

"We'll keep an eagle eye on her," Mr. Jacobs promised.

"Then you stay, I'll go," a defeated Mr. Stevens answered. Whitty and Mina stood watching the men patiently. The room was noiseless.

Mr. Jacobs looked over at Toby once, his jaw tightening. He broke the silence, handing a flashlight over. "Done deal."

The three of them left the room without another word. Toby grabbed Jenna's hand knowing she needed some strength. She smiled weakly up at him.

"We'll get him back Jenna, safe and sound."

Their flashlights shown around the basement but found nothing. When they got to the stairs they stopped and looked at the floor more closely.

"He lost a lot of blood," Jenna said sadly.

"Safe and sound," repeated Toby, squeezing her hand.

"We need to get to the attic where Will found the necklace and skull athame. I think that's where he is. Karl may have more trigger objects there that we don't know about."

They went to the main level, looking a lot like mismatched Charlie's Angels; one with the hair, one with the walkie-talkie, one wishing he had a gun instead of a flashlight. The room was eerily devoid of all life, the uneaten food still out and the music still playing. A clavichord instrumental version of The Holly and the Ivy filled the air.

They searched the room thoroughly and came up empty. Jenna, the only one really familiar with the house, hoped she didn't get lost after all. The three circled around the two main rooms, Jenna knowing another staircase cut into it somewhere. That was the only way she knew how to get to the attic.

"It just opens to the stairs, kinda obscure. I can't find it!"

They had stopped at the door in the red room. Once inside, it had stairs to the immediate right.

"This isn't it?" Mr. Jacobs asked.

Jenna just shook her head. A whining noise was building in her chest with her nerves. She was reaching her breaking point, ready to lose it at any moment, and didn't want an audience.

"Yeah, I need to take a break, a break. Guys, there's a bathroom and I need to take a break," she stammered.

Toby and Mr. Stevens looked back and forth at each other and shrugged. "Okay, we're right here."

Jenna went into the small room and shut the door. She stood at the sink and looked in the mirror. She was surprised to see that she didn't recognize herself. A combination of perpetual fear and apprehension masked her facial features making them the most prominent. Her hands shook as she turned on the faucets. The cold water that splashed her face shocked her into awareness as if she had been sleeping. All at once she stopped, her face dripping wet, chilling her. Something was different, something her subconscious mind detected before her conscious one did. Her heart raced and her eyes were drawn to the other door, the door that opened into the tv room. It was open a crack. Jenna was sure it was closed a moment ago. The flash of movement scared her but caught up too fast for her to grab enough air to scream.

Eighteen

※

ITH ONE ARM, Will grabbed her around her thin waist, pinning her arms to her side. His other hand cupped over her mouth, muffling any attempts at a scream. He had initially started up the stairs to find his mother when a faint image flashed through his mind showing him Jenna and a few others on the main level. Getting her would give him control over everything, so he silently turned around, knowing exactly where to go to cut her off. Her pitstop to the bathroom made it just that much easier.

Will half dragged Jenna backwards out the door he came through, her feet flailing helplessly. She managed to kick once into the door jamb before she disappeared into the room with the cut-in stairs that led to the attic.

"Jenna?"

Outside the room, Mr. Stevens and Toby looked at each other undecided. The noise from inside the bathroom wasn't obviously a yell for help, yet it was a noise. Torn, they were unsure if they should go in or not.

"What's that sound?" Mr. Stevens whispered. He craned his head to listen harder.

"Thumping? Sounds like something being pulled? Jenna! Open up!" Toby pounded on the door once. Despite its solidness, it shook with his strength. He threw open the door to the empty room that now opened into another. The water from the faucet was still running loudly. Toby wrenched the water off and the sounds became clearer.

"Damn it, he has her!" Mr. Stevens bellowed, shoving past Toby, following the clatter now coming from above them.

"Diane, Lee, Will has Jenna and he's heading to the attic!" Toby yelled into the walkie-talkie as he rounded the corners to keep up with Mr. Stevens.

"Be careful! We are all down here waiting, and we are all okay," was the reply. Toby followed from hallway to hallway. He just made it to the top of the attic stairs, out of breath, when he ran into Mr. Stevens who stood there frozen. In the dim light that shown down was Will holding the skull athame to Jenna's neck.

"Now that we have an audience, let's show our hands. Where's the missing piece?"

"I don't have it," Jenna managed to say. Her wide eyes looked from her father to Toby, pleading for help.

"No, I cannot believe that. You came with the ones I needed and the door was opened."

"Yes, I did. Ow. Will, don't, please. You're hurting me."

Will's expression changed so drastically both Mr. Stevens

and Toby's mouths popped open. Will started to ease his stance but started grunting and gasping, his face getting redder and redder as if he was choking on something. He readjusted the athame, his bloody knuckles growing white. He closed his eyes, his face pained. "Jenna," he whispered in her ear. "Where is it?"

"She doesn't have it! Let her go!" her father begged. He stood with his hands out, the beam of light shining brightly on a concentrated spot on the floor. He was ready to jump at any second.

"We can take you to where it is," Toby offered quickly.

Will shot a glance at Toby, doubtful, but interested. It was the only opportunity Mr. Stevens would get. He lunged toward Will to knock him over with the butt of the flashlight. Will raised the hand with the athame and moved to avoid the hit, pushing Jenna in front of himself just as the athame came down, catching the middle of her back. She screamed and fell face first onto the floor. She tried to turn over but Will was on top of her, his knee against her back, his hand again to her neck. Her hair was pulled taut behind her exposing the athame, now dangerously close to her throat. Mr. Stevens stopped and moved away from his daughter.

"You don't even have the piece, do you?" Will taunted Toby.

"It's like a river stone, brown with black and white," Jenna struggled to say in between gasps. She tasted blood and knew she had split her lip. Will released her hair, his hand stroking over the hole in her shirt. Shock crossed his face when his hand came back red. He rubbed her back again gently, his face again straining, turning purple, his eyes bulging.

"Where is it?" he ordered with effort. His voice cracked as he spoke.

"I left it downstairs where I found it. Will, I love you."

Will's jaw clenched. "Show me!" He stood fluidly, pulling Jenna up roughly, his eyes never leaving Toby or Mr. Stevens. The static on Toby came to life.

"Toby, update."

Will eyed the walkie talkie suspiciously. Toby moved only to press the button on the side of the box. "We found it, Diane." He hesitated. "Five minutes, be safe."

"Show me," Will repeated, nodding toward the door. The men hesitantly went back downstairs, never leaving more than a few feet between themselves and Jenna. Her knees wobbled as she took the steps unevenly with Will right at her neck. Every few seconds Will would rub her back absentmindedly followed by the sound of sharp grunts. Jenna noted while passing the main floor the picture windows were still white. The storm outside raged on. It was a long way to the basement and everyone was silent.

My wait at last is over! The amulet, my onyx stone, and athame are necessary for the incantation to be set in motion. Once everything is together the words will come to you to speak regardless of your will. Sylvia's athame would have fortified the spell but the longer we dawdle, the higher the chance this will be bungled. When the spell is completed, my power will eradicate your essence and you will be my vessel. I will seamlessly overtake your mind and continue with the mission. Your youth will afford me many years—

Will had stopped in the kitchen in front of the basement

stairs. He stared at the open door, horrified by Karl's disclosure. "I'm so sorry, Jenna" he whispered, the "a" of her name turning into a moan as he panted for breath. He forcibly pushed her forward. They reached the bottom of the steps near the small pool of blood. Wil regarded it for a long moment before continuing towards the canning cellar. "Where are my aunts and my mother?" he asked apprehensively.

"Your aunts are upstairs with your mom, where they've been all night," Mr. Stevens answered evenly, moving the ray of light from the floor to his face.

"I need to be sure—," Will started to say. He was cut off abruptly once again.

Toby gripped the canning cellar door handle and opened it slowly. He hoped he understood that all the women were together, now waiting on them. Then, as one, they could take Will down. Toby steadied himself to turn backwards to grab him at any second.

Will's plan was kicked into high gear. Will knew the more he thought about what he was going to do the faster he would be stopped by the force within. Without trying to think of anything specific, he skimmed over what he absolutely needed to know before continuing. He just needed to be sure of a few things first.

Within the next few minutes several things took place, acknowledged by the mind in slow motion. The door opened to brighter light where an altar could be seen. It was set up and ready. Will had started to mourn the fact that he would never see his family again, but was incredibly relieved to see them all before him. His gaze touched on everyone in the room, including Mr. Jacobs. All four of his aunts were within his sight, surrounding the altar or standing to the side of the door. His eyes, searching frantically, finally saw his mother—worried and anxious – but safe, standing off to the side, wringing her hands. The cut on Jenna's back didn't seem life threatening so he made peace that he hadn't injured her too badly. That had been too close. He would not allow it to ever happen again.

He was sure the men would take him out, which would just make this that much easier to do. His options were sorely limited, and now the moment of reckoning had come. His heartrate sped up and his breathing increased. Never in a million years would he have thought this was how he was going to leave this mortal world. He hoped he would still be allowed in the Summerland, their heaven. But there was no other way to get rid of Karl. Karl would not allow a banishing ceremony or any spell to be completed other than his own. He had said he would punish anyone who had moved on from a loved one's death. That definitely meant his mom, as well as two of his aunts. There was no way he would allow his body to kill his mother. He needed to move fast before there was time for Karl to catch on. These thoughts—more disjointed in his mind— passed in a millisecond just as his air supply started to dry up.

What are you…?

"Go! Stop this!" Will choked out, pushing Jenna hard in front of him. His air was gone and his face grew red. Already there were white sparkles floating in his field of vision. He saw Toby push his sleeves up and turn around, a look of worry and determination on his face as Will heard Toby yell for the men to grab him.

Quicker than he thought possible, they started to ascend on

him. He backed up with his right hand outstretched in a feeble attempt to keep them away from him to buy that precious moment he needed so badly to do what had to be done.

All the pieces are here!

Without forewarning, a deep growl escaped Will's mouth, so uncharacteristic of him the men faltered. Will's left hand gripped the athame hard and secure. The edge whizzed through the air at the people Will regarded as friends. It moved so fast, the tip caught the meaty part below Toby's thumb, drawing blood instantly.

Will pushed past the resistance he knew he would feel and drew the knife towards himself. His arm jerked away and his body followed as if it wasn't told ahead of time. Mr. Jacobs tried to rush him but the athame followed much to closely to his boss's heart to be safe. All the while there was yelling and crying.

"Mina, start the spell, start the spell!"

"Dad, why is his face that color?"

"Someone get that necklace off him!"

Words bubbled up on Will's lips and he heard his voice start to speak. He pulled as much of his magical abilities as he could to shield it and shrieked. It was a sound so loud and terrifying, the men hesitated again, their faces reflecting confusion and second guessing. Jenna reached into Will's personal space and pulled hard on the onyx necklace. It broke with a snap just as Will hissed, his stare that of pure hatred. She jumped back in defense and threw it into the tiny cauldron to join Sylvia's athame. The bell, citrine crystal, and the amulet surrounded the cauldron.

Will's eyes bugged out as he saw the contents of the altar. A look of desperate determination replaced his fear and terror as female voices started to invoke a spell in unison. Will pinched his lips together as that urge reared up again, stronger than before. He was already moving with the athame in a way that protected his body and kept the others at bay. Now he was beginning to feel the compulsion to attack again and he knew this wasn't going to be just a wave of the blade. He knew it would kill.

"Diane, we need Karl's athame, or this won't work!"

"What is happening to him?"

The time he had bought was fast approaching its end and still his body was locked against his wishes. Will's muscles readied for the deadly strike and he stopped fighting it with as much as he could control. He needed a distraction before all hell broke loose.

"I will speak the words Karl," Will announced, his voice hoarse and cracking.

Immediately, the invisible cage disappeared and he could direct his movements. Sheer joy was replaced with panic before he could even feel it. He found his mouth was moving again. A different kind of triumph coursed through his veins. And this time, part of him wanted to celebrate it. Will used all he had left: the love of his family, to ironically, give him strength to make this right. His sacrifice would be worth it. Hoping it would be enough to overcome Karl, he closed his eyes and quickly brought the sharp blade to his neck, sliding it across his throat as hard as he could. The last thing he heard was Jenna's horrified scream.

"NO!!"

At least she would go on, alive. It was all that really mattered. His family and his love would live, and the evil would die with him. A blanket of red darkness engulfed him, carrying him away from the urge to think, to breathe, to fight.

Nineteen

"NO!!" JENNA SCREAMED again. Several arms grabbed her and pulled her back into the room as she attempted to get to Will. She tried to break free, to see around the men. It looked more like a football tackle mound than an intervention. She needed to see again what could not have been possible to see. She clawed at Mr. Jacobs's shirt to get to Will. Voices were everywhere, yelling, shouting. Emotions surrounded them. Bodies moved frantically.

"Grab something then!" Jenna heard someone yelled.

"Put it right here! Get her off him!"

"Quick, take the athame! Light that sucker up!"

"Oh my dear Goddess, is he breathing?!"

"Move out of the way!"

"How bad is it? Will, open your eyes!"

"Where are we on the parchment?"

"Come on, light the candle!"

"What if he's still Karl?"

"Save Will! He's in there!" Jenna found herself yelling to anyone who would listen. "He would never have said he was sorry or rubbed my back if it were Karl. Will hasn't worried about me in weeks for anything that has hurt me. I'm telling you, he's in there!" Her voice cut out and she sat on the damp floor alone, her face wet with tears. She curled her legs in and hugged them tightly with her arms. It made her back throb, but she didn't care.

Toby and Mr. Stevens were scuffing backward into the room, pulling Will. Several women were tending to him. Mina and Diane lit the candles on the second try their hands were shaking so badly.

Sulis grabbed Jenna's arm to get her up off the floor. "We need you to do this. Come on Jenna, you need to focus right now. Please get up!"

Jenna made it to her feet, following direction. Karl's athame had been added to the cauldron. Everyone now stood forming a circle around the altar. Lee was the only exception, kneeling with one hand over Will's neck with the scarf Whitty had been wearing earlier. Wild faces and flabbergasted expressions matched everyone's soiled and bloodied clothes.

Jenna didn't want to look at Will's body by the altar, but couldn't help it. His eyes were closed. His hair was stuck to his face and his forehead, and he was covered in blood. Bruises had already started to form on his cheek and nose. He was so still she couldn't tell at first if he was breathing.

The old parchment was picked up and everyone was told to put their hands on it. Diane and Mina did their best to read the writing on the faded paper. They followed the instructions to the letter. The lantern's light dimmed and disappeared.

"What happened?" Mr. Stevens asked.

"Battery drain," Diane answered. "It's happens a lot with electronics. Just keep going, the candles are bright enough."

The coven's athames that were on the altar were picked up and touched. The tips emitted small green sparks which made everyone cry out in surprise. As instructed, the blades were raised then lowered, and the sparks settled into a green glow. The glow elongated, reaching across the cauldron several times to connect with each sister.

"Is the light connecting us in triangles?" Lee asked, looking up from the floor. She still had one hand on Will's neck while the other was raised with her athame.

"No, it's connecting the five of us by a pentagram," Sulis realized.

"Look at the cauldron!" Toby exclaimed. The skulls and spiders on the athame in the cauldron pulsed a lighter green, giving the impression they were alive. The group continued with the spell, the power in the room building.

"My whole body is tingling," Jenna shouted. Heads nodded all around.

Will started to twitch, groaning. Lee had to work at keeping the scarf on the wound on his neck. The women spoke faster. The last words were uttered and a thickness filled the room making it stifling hot and hard to breathe. The amulet took on an intense green glow, the depth of color uneven because of its natural pigmentation.

"What the—?" Toby began to ask.

Will suddenly arched and lifted as being pulled upwards from his stomach, his arms and legs still flaccid.

"Lee, you'll need to move away from Will. I'm not sure what's happening," Whitty admitted, a frantic look on her face.

Lee tilted her head at her sisters, desperate, but backed up. She switched the scarf to her the hand holding her athame and stared at her bare palm. It was red but not dripping. "Not a lot of blood!" The red holiday scarf did little to indicate the severity of his cut. She lifted it towards the nearest candle, the tension in her shoulders easing. "It's not soaked. The bleeding slowed."

Will moaned loudly and his eyes opened. The pulsing light of the skulls and athames quickened, the green leaching out to a dull white that took on a sickly hue. That same hue seemed to envelope Will as well, vague at first, then rising from beneath him to his surface.

"NO!" Will howled. The body was his. The voice was not. "No!" The words became garbled as Will's face and torso shifted and morphed.

The air in the room drew down in a vortex towards Will. The weight caused everyone to bend over abruptly.

"I can't breathe," stammered Toby.

Without warning, the air blasted upward, pushing everyone back on their heels as an image emerged out of Will with the turbulence. It was ashen—an unhealthy white like the sallowness of a fish long washed ashore—with a faint green lining the edges. As it grew in size, the green was squeezed out. The shape took on distinctive features as the air pressure in the room changed once again and the temperature plummeted several degrees.

"That's the man I've been seeing!" Jenna shouted. Everyone else continued to chant the final section of the spell. Diane held the amulet over the candle.

Without warning, Karl's washed-out likeness shot up, enraged and magnified to four times normal size. It filled the small room and rushed at a screaming Jenna just as Diane dropped the flaming amulet in with the skull athame.

Green blinding light blew out from the cauldron, overtaking everything in the candlelit room. It connected with the green energy link between the women and grew into a cone that began at their feet and continued upward in a spiral funnel. The icy air pulled away from the corners and brushed past everyone as it was sucked into the cauldron along with the image of Karl. The candles blew out just as a loud pop made the earth under their feet shake. A red fire flamed from the cauldron, crackling loudly, consuming stone and metal. It soon died down, almost as quickly as it appeared.

"Where are your backup lights?" Toby's voice asked in the darkness. There was more noise and yelling as things were being tipped over and plastic was clacking against itself. The striking of a match was heard and the faintest of lights lit the room.

"The flashlights are all dead," Whitty said.

"Is everyone all right?" Mina asked. Some grunted, some answered. Jenna immediately went to Will, bumping into Sulis and Lee. He moved slowly on the floor groaning louder now.

He muttered, unintelligibly. The first discernable words were names, repeating over and over.

Sulis pushed the collar of his shirt apart, her fingers visibly shaking. His neck had a superficial cut from just under his right ear to the end of his right jawbone. It was still bleeding, but it had slowed down considerably on its own.

"It's not as bad as we thought it would be," Lee announced, relieved, her hand to her chest. Will was arousing. Jenna brushed back the dark hair that always seemed to be in his eyes.

"Your mom is here, and your aunts are here. I'm right here, Will. Talk to me, tell me it's you," Jenna whispered. "Are you okay?"

Will's eyes opened and he looked around, confused. He focused on Jenna for a few seconds before recognition hit him. Then he frowned, reaching his hand up towards her face. She cringed at first, not sure what he would do. Several sets of hands were on her shoulders and next to her in an instant in case he meant to harm her. Will hesitated; his arm stopped in midair, a disgusted look on his face as he slowly continued to her and ran his finger across her swollen lips.

"I'm not sure. Am I okay? Who else did I hurt?" His voice was thick and raspy but getting clearer, settling into the soft-spoken tone that was completely Will. Jenna hoped he would keep talking; it felt like home.

Sulis ran her hand over his shoulder. "We're fine, Will. Holy Mother Earth you scared us!" she cried. "No parent should ever see something like that. What were you thinking? What happened?"

"Karl had a good foothold. Any time I tried to do what I

wanted that conflicted with his plans, he cut off my air supply. I figured I wouldn't make it out alive anyway if you made it through a spell to get rid of him. I certainly wasn't going to be my own person had he gone through with his plans. This body refused to do his dirty business anymore." He paused. "Why am I still alive anyway? I thought I would have done myself in."

"It was utterly horrific to watch, but it was like watching two people fight. You raised your arm but it went back down. You raised it again, strained against it actually, and put the knife, well... You didn't exert as much force as you meant to. I don't think it cut too deeply if it's almost stopped bleeding on its own. It might not even leave a noticeable scar."

"Will, Dad and I are happy you're okay," Toby said, helping the others clean off the altar. "Even if it looks like you went a few rounds with a heavy weight. Over here Mr. Stevens. That can go in this bag."

"Sissy, come look at this," Diane called.

"Absolutely." Sulis turned back to her son. "It looks like you're in good hands now anyway."

Will touched his neck tenderly, then his head from when he fell earlier in the night. His eyes never left Jenna's.

"What can I do to show you how sorry I am for what I've put you through?"

"I just need to know it's only you in there." Jenna paused. "And don't ever wear your hair in a ponytail, okay?"

Jenna shifted to help Will sit up. His jaw tightened once again, his eyes hungrily searching hers, taking in every nuance in appreciation.

"You can't possibly know how excruciating it's been to have

you there and not be able to touch you, help you. Sometimes I didn't even realize how cruel I was." He closed his eyes in regret.

"S'okay now. I knew that wasn't you."

He opened his eyes once again, freed, his breathing speeding up. "Thank you." He reached out tentatively, running his hand down her face, touching her lips, under her hair to the back of her head. His hand came back, down her shoulder to her collarbone. Using both hands now, he slid them through her hair and pulled her to him. The kiss was gentle, controlled, but very passionate. Jenna's reservations to protect herself melted as she kissed him, her forceful reply the weeks of pent up frustration channeled into relief.

There were several uncomfortable coughs coming from next to them, then gasps. Diane, Mina, and Whitty were pulling the items out of the cauldron now. The necklace was nothing more than the stone. But now, somehow, the onyx was even more pronounced in color, blacker than midnight. Karl's athame had shattered in two places. The metal had melted just enough to blend the skulls and faces into a smear of indiscernible lumps. The moonstone was a deep iridescent scarlet as if a fire was contained inside. The amulet was only a blackened stone. Sulis removed the two pieces of Sylvia's athame, holding each gingerly.

"I can't believe the wooden handle is still intact," Mr. Jacobs admitted, shaking his head.

"Charred, but there," Sulis added. "Both athames have been broken. I think it's safe to say whatever magic was held in them is now gone."

"Agreed," Mina said.

"Mina, did we do it?" Mr. Stevens asked.

"Yes, I think we did. How do you feel Sulis?"

Her sister looked down in embarrassment. "I'm ashamed to say how far this got and how far it almost went. I can't believe how obvious it is now what I was doing, when just a few days ago it seemed to make so much sense. It never even fazed me that warning bells should have gone off when Will gave me Sylvia's athame. But I feel like my old self. This is the first ritual I've been to with that much power. Or one that's turned into a self-intervention."

"Where did Karl go? Why was he here in the first place?" Toby asked.

"I think we need to do some more research to find out all the answers. Now that Sulis and Will are back, maybe they can enlighten us. So this doesn't ever repeat," added Diane, hugging her baby sister. "It looks like we won't need to do any other spells tonight. That one was a whopper."

"I have no urge to find anything or do anything other than maybe sleep for a week," Sulis admitted.

"I'm exhausted as well, mom. And I need to piece together what the heck I've been doing the last month."

"We'll all sleep better knowing you both are okay," Mina said quietly. She turned away to wipe the stray tears that insisted on falling.

"I'm interested in knowing where all these talismans will be going. Is there such a thing as a safe place? I don't want to lose sleep over a stone being rubbed the wrong way or a nail being touched twice bringing back more of this," Mr. Stevens confessed. "And I certainly won't want to worry about anything too tempting that inquisitive minds find hard to resist," he said pointedly at Will.

Mr. Stevens wasn't too upset with Will, though. He couldn't hold a grudge against him. He was more than certain the guy wasn't acting on his own behalf. What bothered him the most now was the way his daughter looked at the boyfriend when he kissed her. Mr. Stevens sighed. He always knew the time would come when he wouldn't worry about her finding the wrong man, but finding the right one. And just like most dads, he thought he had more time.

Twenty

AFTER THE ADRENALINE died down and everything remained normal, everyone quietly finished cleaning up. Jenna, Will, and Toby went to the bottom of the stairs to wipe up the blood before making their way to the food table. It gave the adults a chance to talk.

"What *was* going through your mind these last few weeks, Sissy?" Mina asked Sulis.

Sulis shook her head, dumbfounded. "The need to find that citrine crystal and apparently not much else. I seemed to go through my day on rote, doing what my usual day would entail, although some of that was slipping away as well. I forgot to finish laundry and prepare nutritious meals. Will was busy doing his own thing, which I now realize was at Karl's direction. He wasn't acting oddly to me. I did not see this coming." She stopped to take a huge breath of air.

"You were preoccupied," Lee agreed, putting her arm on her sister's shoulder. "That must have been very scary."

"The more I think about it, the scarier it becomes. When Will gave me Sylvia's athame, something inside my head felt complete at the same time I yearned for more," Sulis continued.

"You didn't stop to think why Will had it now when it had disappeared when we closed the window on Halloween night?" Mr. Jacobs asked, confusion coloring his words more than anything.

"No, I did not. Then, a few days ago, Will showed me the other athame and told me what we were to do with it when Jenna came over tonight. It was perfectly logical to me. He told me she had both the bell and the crystal—"

"How would he know that? He didn't know that," Mr. Stevens interrupted. Both he and Mr. Jacobs were shocked and looked nervous. The women nodded sagely at the extent this had manifested.

"We can never underestimate the power of a dark mind that practices magic and what that man was capable of," Diane said.

"Well, nothing else turned up in the altar room," Whitty said, coming out from the cubby area and handing her sister a notebook. "I scoured every nook. It's clean. I jotted down the markings on the runes for you, Diane, so you can translate."

Mr. Stevens glanced at the elder sister.

"I'm the only one in our coven who is familiar with runes." Diane reviewed the paper. "There is nothing new from these symbols that we don't already know. Sylvia and Karl must have marked the door with the only thing they could that couldn't be read by a layperson or interpreted as something that related to witches. The room itself was hidden quite well. No one had discovered it for over a hundred years."

"True. It would have been longer if Will wasn't such a twig," Whitty agreed.

After the altar items were put back in Mina's satchel and the makeshift altar returned to its home in the middle of the cellar, they all made their way back upstairs to the kitchen. The dining room table had been cleared off with empty plates stacked by the sink. Jenna was transferring the last of the leftovers into storage containers and handing them to Will for the fridge. Both were working around Toby who was wolfing down food just as quickly as they were saving it.

Sulis walked over to her son and hugged him tightly. "Don't ever let me see something like that again." She continued on and hugged Jenna. "Thank you," she said simply.

Once the house was put back in order, they all attended to their minor cuts and scrapes. Will was, by far, the worse off, after wrestling all the men into the hidden room, and falling down the stairs. He looked much better after a shower, but the bruises would take weeks before they'd fade. The slash on his neck wasn't serious and a very relieved Sulis declared how happy she was not to have to make a trip to the hospital in the bad weather.

It was after midnight before everyone started to plop onto the chairs in the green room to relax. All Will's aunts had somehow squeezed themselves onto the couch. Mr. Stevens sat in the accent chair and rubbed his eyes. Jenna sat close by him, finding a place with Will on the fluffy rug together, their hands entwined and their heads resting against each other. They spoke quietly in their own little world. Jenna's free hand would occasionally find its way up to his shoulder where he would lean over and hug her tightly. At other times he would stare at her, his finger caressing her skinned lip which led to them kissing. From across the room, Toby nestled a cup of hot cocoa in between his legs and watched Will with apprehension. Mr. Stevens realized he was a good friend. He always watched out for Jenna.

Mr. Jacobs pulled back the thick living room curtain after turning on the walkway light and looked at the blizzard outside. No longer a whiteout, the winds had died down and the worse seemed over. The roads out front were completely covered and hard to discern where they actually were. No snowplows had been through yet this late at night, not that uncommon in their small town. It was still snowing, except now the large fluffy flakes that fell lazily from the sky were no longer threatening. According to the accumulation in the driveway and on top of the large white mounds that were cars, they had received over two feet of snow since they arrived.

"I hope this isn't going to be awkward, staying over," Sulis worried. She had changed into jogging pants and t-shirt, and had pulled over a dining room chair to sit.

"We told our wives it was more like a Christmas party for the Historical Association members. Not too far off, really," Mr. Jacobs said, coming back from the window. "And you can't drive on roads that aren't there."

The aroma of fresh brewed coffee coming from the kitchen helped to break the image of the night's incidents. Once everyone was together, Toby shifted and took out of his pocket the list of words Jenna had written while asleep late that one night. For the first time, Sulis and her sisters were able to look it over.

Bell tell hell door more store Dual Yule fuel Find mind bind
Bell tell hell door more store Dual Yule fuel Find mind bind
Bell tell hell door more store Dual Yule fuel Find mind bind

BRRS APG
EEIK WSNY

"I can surmise what the rhyming words stand for, but the code at the bottom has me dumbfounded," Diane replied, looking over the paper she had placed on her lap. Her hands were curled around a large mug of steaming black coffee.

"Sure, the words "bell" and "tell" are obvious," Mina said, leaning over and chewing the end of her eyeglasses.

"I think I have a good idea about what "hell" implies," Mr. Stevens admitted, when the paper made its way to him. His face still wrinkled with the events of the night.

"The "door" must be about the canning cellar's door," said Toby as he rubbed the back of his hand where Will had cut him as he was forced into the small room.

"It very well could mean a figurative door that allowed the magic to cross over to us," Lee offered. Everyone bobbed their heads at that real possibility.

"Someone please tell me the word "more" isn't warning me there will be more," Mr. Jacobs begged as he set his cup on the wooden table to take the paper.

The room was silent for a moment and everyone tried to find a logical meaning behind the word.

"Well, we've had more than our share with this whole thing. There were so many people involved and it did continue for quite a while." Mr. Stevens tried to rationalize the word on the paper with a definite answer. It was too vague.

"I'd like to think the word "store" explains the power of the crystal, bell, necklace, and both Will and Sulis. There was a lot of energy and influence stored in each."

"Yes, you're right, Mina," Diane agreed. "The "dual" could be a few things. The conflict Will and Sulis felt sharing their bodies and minds with a dark entity as well as the confrontation of Will and Karl. What we watched Will do to his neck…"

Sulis shifted uncomfortably and took a very large breath in through her nose before blowing it out slowly. "Yes, there's that. At least "Yule" is self-explanatory. The "fuel" was the desire to find those missing pieces to do Karl's bidding." The group looked up at her apprehensively. She sipped her coffee and nodded firmly. "Trust me."

"The rest seems easy enough. "Find" and "bind" don't really need an explanation," Toby said. "But what I'd like to know is why the citrine crystal was on the bottom of the altar's material. I would never have looked there to find it."

Diane nodded with a small smile. "Back in the day, women used to sew important things into their garments, like coins. Witches sewed their gems and crystals into their skirts to avoid detection, while having them near all the time. Sylvia was clever."

"We didn't realize it when we took the altar apart. I'm really impressed Jenna found it," Toby said, raising his eyebrows at his friend. Jenna blushed.

"Sylvia led me. Mostly through my dreams."

Sulis took another sip. "That not only verifies how talented our lovely Jenna is, it proves how important it is to get her trained in control." Will looked at Jenna with such pride, everyone laughed.

"I think I speak for all of us when I say we'd be happy to help teach her how to use her magical abilities," Mina said. That was when Jenna truly felt she belonged there.

"So, we've decoded most of the words. I would like to try to work on the letters at the bottom of the page. I like puzzles," Toby offered, taking back the list and stuffing it back into his pocket when no one objected.

"Then more power to you, Tobe," his dad agreed tiredly. "You're a smart kid. Now that we have all the pieces, it's just a matter of time before you figure it out."

It seemed there was nothing new to glean from the house or the evening, and everyone was spent. Exhausted, they relaxed for a while with casual conversation before crashing on whatever couch or bed they could find. The storm had passed and the snowplows came out very early in the morning.

"THREE, TWO, ONE, Happy New Year!" the television rang out. The greeting repeated around the room, glasses clinked, and people hugged.

"Did I miss it?" asked Toby, running back into the room, a

gold foil party hat bobbing on his head. His mouth was full of spinach puffs. Two more were in his hands.

"Yes, you did," Sulis said, sitting back down into the deep sofa with her glass of champagne.

"Leave it to you to miss the moment by filling your face," Jenna laughed. She snuggled closer to Will, having barely made it to midnight awake.

"Well, the food is magnificent," Mrs. Jacobs offered in her son's defense. Steph Jacobs was a petite woman with eyes the same color as Toby's. She was dressed well with nicely manicured hair and nails and was friendly and outgoing. She turned to her husband and put her hand on his knee lovingly.

Mr. Jacobs smiled at his wife and agreed. "I second that wholeheartedly."

"Thank you," said Lee and Whitty together. They continued with their conversation from the previous year only minutes before.

"So, Stephanie, I'll check with the instructor but I'm pretty sure there's still space to join that jewelry making class Whitty, Diane, and I are going to. The first class starts in March. Do you want to go?" Lee asked her new friend.

"I sure do, that sounds like fun. Making jewelry is one of the few things I haven't done yet. Plus, I could also add that to my repertoire and include my new creations on my table at the craft fair."

"Ooh, I love crafts!" Whitty exclaimed, her eyes getting wide. Mr. Jacobs just rolled his eyes and smirked.

"You've created a monster," said Lee and Mr. Jacobs at exactly the same time.

"The food is wonderful and so is this house. Honestly, it's one of the few homes I've been in of this size that still has that warm and inviting feel to it," Jenna's mom, Gwen, said. She put her glass down and nestled back into the crook of her husband's arm, the glittery plastic tiara she was wearing whacking him in the nose.

"It's all about restoring and renewing, mom. It's hard work," Jenna stated. Muffled snickers filled the green room. Gwen shrugged off the laughs as reactions to her party favor.

"Thank you so much. I think it does, too." Sulis smiled, looking around room contentedly.

And it had. The last days of December picked up right where they left off at the beginning of the month. Both Will and Sulis reengaged in school, work, and family life. Even though they didn't celebrate Christmas, they did exchange Yule gifts. Jenna actually snorted through her nose when she opened a *Star Trek: The Next Generation* gift. It was a 5x7 cast ensemble photo, prominently featuring Deanna Troi in front.

The events of the Yule ceremony dimmed in everyone's memories. Karl's belongings and the amulet had been gathered with the plan to bury them as soon as the ground thawed in the spring. In the meantime, they would be kept under Sulis's guard, so as not to interact with anything adversely. They agreed the citrine crystal and bell were safe enough to keep. Sylvia's parchment was to be buried as well, after some scrutiny from each to gather as much information as they could, written or implied.

It was also a good sign when Rommy came out from

hiding wherever he had been for the last few weeks and actually jumped up on Will's lap, purring.

It was to be a long, well deserved rest for the remainder of the winter. The spring? That was another story.

Epilogue 1870

"I HEARD HE KILLED a man, Levander, and met a sticky end. Are you sure you want something that belonged to someone like that?"

"It's Mr. Robertson to you, Michael. No matter how old you are, I'm still your elder. And I'm tellin' ya, I want that dang ring and my credit is good here."

"Yes, sir, Mr. Robertson, my apologies." He tried to lighten the mood and a little flattery couldn't hurt. "Your credit has always been good with me, and I hear in town as well."

Mike Snow hated to be put in his place, but he was a businessman and wanted to stay in the chap's good graces. He was his best customer in the store. He also had a big mouth. If something displeased him, it didn't take long before a business felt its wake.

"Pardon me, but why would you want something so," he hesitated, "so odd?"

The ring in question was purposely kept away from the counter and in a corner of the tiny store, on the bottom of a small shelf. It made Mike very uneasy. He would be relieved to unload such an item. He was unhappy the learn the only way to consolidate the owner's lingering debt after he abruptly left was by collecting what remained in his house. Now Mike was stuck with a thick, gold ring with what resembled a very realistic green eyeball in the center. Despite the value, no one came near it.

"It's fer my private collection and stop trying to schmooze me. I might not be older than dirt, but I'm smarter than it." He did look older than thirty-seven and the fact that his mouth held nothing but pink gums did not help.

"Of course." Mike wanted to say more, but the words he wanted to continue with would just rile up the ornery man.

"How'd you know the man killed?"

"What was that? Oh, yes. Well, people talk, sir. He came from the Old Country and hooked up with the Widow Cabet. Only the good Lord knows what they did together. There was some mighty strange stories going around. No one knows why he just up and left. Maybe his past caught up with him. Not everyone trusted James's boarders either, God rest his soul. Shifty characters, the most of them. One can only imagine what that combination did behind closed doors."

Mr. Robertson's mouth clamped down into a frown making his lips nearly disappear. "I said, how do you know he killed, son?"

The answer wouldn't sway Levander from his desire to own the strange ring. He wanted it regardless. The story might give some insight into what it was meant for. Instead of a shiny stone, it held an eye in the very center. It was an eye that seemed to find you no matter where the ring was located. It wouldn't stop him from the need to collect items. His basement was full of them and he remembered the story behind each one.

"Well, sir, rumors circulate. After the string of deaths of those widows and widowers, he left Orchard Creek and went back into town for a time. Someone crossed his path the wrong way from what I heard."

"Is that so?"

"Yes sir. Blew his head clean off. He was grabbed and held by the locals. The dead man's son shot him before the sheriff could arrive."

About the Author

*S*PELL BREAKERS IS the third installment in Laura Livingston Snyder's Infinity Series. The first novel: *Dream Seer*, published in June, 2020, and second novel: *Realm Speaker*, published in October, 2020, satisfies her lifelong goal of being a published author.

Meditations Handbook: Four Revelations of the Solar Wheel of Meditations, Affirmations, and Guided Imagery for Pagan Sabbats is a stand-alone book published in August, 2020, that delves into mindfulness techniques.

Laura is an RN and Certified Case Manager. She has several years of experience as a freelance writer for a local magazine, and occasionally blogs at FreshAppleSnyder.com. She lives in Upstate New York with her husband, children, pets, and lots of gardens.

Watch for *Prism Reader*, the fourth book in the Infinity Series, and other novels coming soon.